The Exclamation

The Exclamation Mark

Anton Chekhov

Translated by Rosamund Bartlett

ET REMOTISSIMA PROPE

Hesperus Classics

Essex County Council Libraries

Hesperus Classics
Published by Hesperus Press Limited
4 Rickett Street, London SW6 1RU
www.hesperuspress.com

First published in Russian, 1885–6
First published by Hesperus Press Limited, 2008

Introduction, selection and English language translation © Rosamund Bartlett
Foreword © Lynne Truss, 2008

Designed and typeset by Fraser Muggeridge studio
Printed in Jordan by the Jordan National Press

ISBN: 978-1-84391-174-6

CONTENTS

FOREWORD

I first came to Chekhov's stories by way of his great admirer (and early advocate), the New Zealand-born short story writer Katherine Mansfield. I was in my early twenties. I had studied Chekhov's plays with a passionate intensity in my third year at university, and I remember with some embarrassment a very keen essay I wrote for my tutor, in which I rather magisterially picked out three instances of characters declaring, tearfully, 'You look so old!' and then floundered about hopelessly, trying to make something of it.

But Chekhov's stories having no place in an English Literature degree at that time, it was only the publication of Katherine Mansfield's *Letters and Journals* in 1977 that made me realise how important they were. What a brilliant critic Katherine Mansfield was. Looking back, I now realise that I've never had reason to quibble with a single one of her sharp – but usually affectionate – literary weighings-up. Of E.M. Forster, for example, Mansfield complains in her journal that he 'never gets any further than warming the teapot. He's a rare fine hand at that. Feel this teapot. Is it not beautifully warm? Yes, but there ain't going to be no tea.' George Gissing's works are written 'with cold wet feet under a wet umbrella.' Meanwhile George Bernard Shaw is 'the concierge in the house of literature – sits in a glass case, sees everything, knows everything, examines the letters, *cleans the stairs*, but has no part, no part in the life that is going on.'

But when she comes to Chekhov (or 'T' for Tchehov, as he appears in her writings), she has only admiration and awe. She finds it unbearable that he is not alive. In the 'house of literature', where George Bernard Shaw wields the mop and bucket, only three writers actually live, she says, and they are all Russian: 'Dostoevsky, Tchehov and Tolstoy. I can't think of *anyone else*.' And she defends this position very convincingly. Helping her friend S.S. Koteliansky with an edition of Chekhov's letters, in 1919 she re-reads his magnificent 'The Steppe' (1888) and writes: 'One feels about this story not that it *becomes* immortal – it always was. It has no beginning or end. T. just touched one point with his pen, and then another point – *enclosed* something which had, as it were, been there for ever.'

What initially put me off his stories, I think, was that there were so damned many of them, and I didn't know where to start. Also, the collections in paperback seemed completely random in their selection, which gave me a feeling of vertigo whenever I picked up a new one. True, I bought *The Kiss and Other Stories*, *The Duel and Other Stories*, *Lady with Lapdog and Other Stories*, *The Russian Master and Other Stories* – and I still have those books, but they have always made me a bit uneasy simply because the organising principle isn't clear. 'The ten stories in this collection were written between 1887 and 1902,' the blurb might offer, and I'd think, 'But that means they span virtually his whole career! What makes these ones go together, then?' Each new collection just compounded the difficulty. 'The eleven stories in *this* collection were written between 1885 and 1899' another blurb would say, and I would start to roll my eyes in panic. Chronology might not mean a lot to some readers, but it means a lot to me. Given Chekhov's tragically short but unbelievably fruitful and varied career, it's arguable that a clear chronology is something to be clung to at all times.

So what a treat this collection is. As Rosamund Bartlett explains in the introduction, these stories were all written by Chekhov in a six-month period, and to anthologise them in this way, in order of composition, is to shine a light on a period in his writing (December 1885 to June 1886) that is generally considered to represent a turning point. It was in March 1886 that Chekhov received a momentous letter from the famous writer Dmitry Grigorovich, exhorting him to aim higher than the throwaway comic pieces he was writing for lightweight periodicals. He took it to heart. A month after the correspondence with Grigorovich comes the terrifically visual and moving 'On Easter Night' – a story which perfectly illustrates Katherine Mansfield's point, actually. One feels that the genius of the writer here is to note a story that was always there (and always would be) and to enclose it with those wand-like touches of the pen.

What we see in this collection is Chekhov's complex literary sensibility with all its facets sparkling (as it were) quite separately, in an incredibly useful way for anyone who wants to understand this most misunderstood of writers. Here we see him learning to control and combine a somewhat wild array of writerly instincts and skills, while still apparently churning out stories at the rate of one a day. 'New Year Martyrs' may be just a throwaway sketch, but it has great comic timing, and I laughed every time the policeman piped up, 'Another civil servant has been brought in!' This is a great comic playwright at work in the columns of a newspaper. 'A Nightmare' ends with a bathetic crash ('So began and ended the genuine inclination to useful activity of one well-intentioned but thoroughly complacent and not terribly thought-ful person'), which shows authorial panache, I suppose, but is surely unworthy of the story that precedes it. But the exciting sense through-out is: Chekhov is deliberately mixing it up. He is in transition, but he is never not in control. He is making the world his own. And he is – easy to forget this – just 26 years old.

In her wonderful book *Reading Chekhov* (2003), Janet Malcolm offers an outstandingly helpful analysis of the effect of the great stories. She says that they may have a 'straightforward, natural, rational, mod-ern surface' but that this 'bark of the prosaic' is used by Chekhov to encase the story's 'vital poetic core, *as if such protection were necessary for its survival* [my italics].' I would recommend any reader of this collection to watch out for this encasing process taking place – but also, obviously, to enjoy the sheer variety of tone and effect Chekhov was engaged in over such a short period. His punctuation-as-apparition Christmas story 'The Exclamation Mark' has a special place in my heart, for obvious reasons, but I suggest you compare it with 'On Easter Night' and then ask yourself how much *you've* ever managed to move on in any six-month period of your own life.

– *Lynne Truss, 2008*

This anthology differs from most other Chekhov collections in that it concentrates on relatively early stories, and on stories written over a short time-span, namely the six months between the end of December 1885 and the end of June 1886. Chekhov published sixty-two stories during this period, in five different publications: about a third of them are included here. Arranged in chronological order, they enable us to follow in some detail Chekhov's creative evolution at a very interesting point in his career, when he was already popular, but not yet a literary celebrity. It was during this six-month period that Chekhov published a story under his own name for the first time, received a momentous letter from a celebrated contemporary author exhorting him to take his writing more seriously, and published his first major short story collection, which he called *Motley Tales*. This brought Chekhov to the attention of Russia's most important literary journals, whose critics found his irony and moral neutrality immediately threatening. Their first reviews of Chekhov's stories were almost uniformly negative. Nevertheless, it was clear also that here was a writer developing into a serious talent, and invitations to contribute to these august publications soon followed.

In the first half of 1886, Chekhov was still mostly writing 'lightweight' stories for the lowbrow comic journals with which he had made his name. Accordingly, the majority of the twenty stories included in this anthology are humorous, and thus counter the clichéd and strangely resilient view of Chekhov as an exclusively gloomy writer. The reason Chekhov first achieved literary success was because he made Russian readers laugh. 'The Exclamation Mark', for example, the story which opens this collection, is an insouciant piece which is entirely typical of Chekhov's early period. At a Christmas Eve party, collegiate secretary Efim Fomich Perekladin, with forty years' service as a government functionary behind him, is challenged on his educational background by one of the other guests. Since the young man's father, as a collegiate counsellor, occupies a higher position in the all-important Table of Ranks, Perekladin can only bite his lip and smile meekly, but he is incensed at being criticised by someone so much younger than him. At home in bed later that night, he mentally gives vent to his feelings of indignation, but as soon as he falls asleep, the more deeply seated feelings of insecurity in his unconscious take over and he starts dreaming of punctuation marks… There was no possibility of Chekhov himself using punctuation marks unconsciously after he had written this story, which was included in *Motley Tales* (as was 'Grief', also anthologised here). Indeed, his idiosyncratic use of punctuation, whose importance he later compared to 'notes in a musical score', was to become a hallmark of his mature literary style. Its most notable feature is his increasingly lyrical use of ellipses, '…', at the end of sentences and paragraphs, which amounts to the prose equivalent of the crucially important pauses inserted into his last plays. It is seen to best effect in this collection in the much longer 'On Easter Night', which is also artistically one of the most impressive stories Chekhov wrote in 1886.

Chekhov was not only adept at writing about civil servants and monks. The stories in this selection alone feature a large cast of characters of varying ages, backgrounds and occupations, including very small children, cab drivers, drunkards, writers, landowners, musicians, nubile girls, rooks and flies. The settings are also diverse, including toboggan runs, ferries, dachas, St Petersburg streets, dining room tables and newspaper pages. Chekhov gives his reader a pretty good cross-section of Russian life. One of the advantages of concentrating on one specific period in Chekhov's career, moreover, is that we can see him deftly and sometimes quite abruptly changing his literary personality from story to story, depending on the publication he is writing for.

Half the stories in this collection were written for the St Petersburg-based *Fragments* ('*Oskolki*'), which was Russia's most popular comic weekly in the 1880s. Chekhov started writing for it in 1882, and, under a variety of pseudonyms, soon became its star author. He wrote initially because he needed the money to support his impecunious family (his father had gone bankrupt), and subsequently because he was under contract, with strict deadlines and word-counts, and an obligation to entertain. The *Fragments* stories and vignettes were often extremely witty, but not always. None of them were intended to be anything other than ephemeral, but sometimes they were frivolous to the point of being quite ridiculous. Into this category fall items such as 'On the

Telephone', 'The Rook', 'The Literary Table of Ranks' and 'A Tale'. It is indicative that Chekhov excluded over half of the *Fragments* stories in this collection when he came to edit his writings for his collected works at the end of his life, but they have been deliberately, and unusually, included here in order to give a full sense of the texture of his creative life as it evolved in early 1886. It is also partly for this reason that these 'lesser' works have been preferred to other better-known stories published during this six-month period, such as 'Night at the Cemetery', 'Anyuta', 'The Witch', 'Agafya' and 'The Privy Counsellor'.

When he wrote his famous letter in March 1886, the writer Dmitry Grigorovich demanded that Chekhov honour the talent that had become noticeable in the stories he was commissioned to write for the *Petersburg Newspaper* from May 1885 onwards. In fact it is clear from the three *Petersburg Newspaper* stories included here ('Kids', 'Grief' and 'Spring Time') that Chekhov had started taking greater care even before receiving the letter which he declared had struck him like a 'bolt of lightning'. Chekhov sometimes signed his *Fragments* stories 'The Brother of My Brother' or 'The Man Without a Spleen', but for the *Petersburg Newspaper* he always used his best-known pseudonym 'Antosha Chekhonte'. Quite apart from anything else, Chekhov did not want to harm his professional reputation as a doctor of medicine: he was still practising at this time, having only graduated in the summer of 1884.

Although he came from the provinces, Chekhov based himself happily in Moscow as an adult, along with his poverty-stricken family. His first visit to the Russian capital in December 1885 as an up-and-coming writer was a big event in his life, however, and was reflected immediately in two stories with St Petersburg settings: 'New Year Martyrs' and 'Grief'. It was during this visit that Chekhov was also commissioned to write for Russia's most prominent daily newspaper, *New Times* ('*Novoe vremya*'). 'The Requiem', published in February 1886, was the first story Chekhov published under his own name, and demonstrates to perfection his gift for mixing comedy with tragedy. Along with 'A Nightmare' and 'On Easter Night', the two other *New Times* stories included in this collection, it is also from an artistic point of view far more substantial than anything he had written to date.

Indeed it is instructive to juxtapose something as slight as 'The Rook', published on 29th March in *Fragments,* with the harrowing story 'A Nightmare', published on the same day in *New Times.*

If Chekhov changed his literary personality to suit the publication he was writing for, he was also sensitive to the rhythms of daily life in Russia, and his stories were often highly topical. A final reason for the decision to anthologise stories from the six-month period December 1885 to June 1886 is that it enables us to trace the path of the Russian seasons. Like Chekhov's readers, we can live via his stories through the heavy snow of the long, harsh winter, and eventually experience the thaw, when the ice melts, the rivers swell, the rooks traditionally return to the cities, the sun shines once again, and the roads turn to thick mud. The long-awaited onset of spring is then rapidly followed by summer, which means dacha season. 'Superfluous People', one of Chekhov's many stories about dacha life, was of course itself written at a dacha.

Chekhov's early fiction was not only often closely tied to the season in which it was published, but to the customs associated with imperial Russia's major festivals and holidays, such as Christmas and New Year, reflected in 'The Exclamation Mark', and 'New Year Martyrs', when government flunkeys had unfailingly to sign obsequious greetings cards to their superiors, and pay endless visits to their friends and colleagues. The most important festival, however, was always Easter, preceded by the revelries of Russian Shrovetide, with its ritual of pancake-eating, lovingly described by Chekhov in 'Bliny', and then the seven weeks of Great Lent. Easter in Russia begins on the stroke of midnight with the lighting of candles, the pealing of bells, singing and processions round the church. Chekhov's story 'Easter Night' must rank as one of the most moving evocations of its celebration ever written.

Chekhov typically made very slight revisions to his stories when later preparing them for publication in his collected works. A rare exception is the tobogganing story 'A Little Joke', first published in March 1886. When revising it in 1899, Chekhov decided to turn the garrulous, self-confident narrator into a person who is far more sensitive and less assured. The narrative tone becomes accordingly more understated and elegiac, while the story's ending is changed so drastically that the later version is appended here in its entirety. Comparing it with the less well-known earlier version which, like other stories in this collection, has never before been translated into English, gives us a bird's-eye view of Chekhov's path to creative maturity.

– Rosamund Bartlett, 2008

The Exclamation Mark

Collegiate Secretary Efim Fomich Perekladin[1] went to bed on Christmas Eve feeling offended and even insulted.

'Leave me alone, you old witch!' he barked at his wife when she asked him why he was being so grumpy.

The fact is that he had just returned from a party where many things had been said which he found unpleasant and offensive. At first they had talked in general about the benefits of education, then imperceptibly they had switched to discussing the educational qualifications of government employees, and moreover had expressed many regrets and reproachs and even gibes about low standards. And then, as always happens in Russian social gatherings, from the general they had turned to the particular.

'Well, let's take you, for example, Efim Fomich,' said one young man, turning to Perekladin. 'You have a decent position... What education did you receive?'

'None whatsoever. But you don't need to have education in our department,' said Perekladin meekly. 'You just have to write correctly, and that's all there is to it...'

'But where did you learn to write correctly?'

'Well, it's practice, isn't it?.. You get to become quite a dab hand when you have been on the payroll for forty years... It is true it was hard at the beginning, and I used to make mistakes, but then I learned the ropes and... it's fine now...'

'But what about punctuation marks?'

'And punctuation marks aren't a problem... I put them in the right places.'

'Hmm!..' said the young man, abashed. 'All the same, practice is not the same as education. It's all very well you putting punctuation marks in the right places. But that's only half of it! You have to be aware of how you use them! When you insert a comma, you have to know why... Yes indeed! As for your unconscious, reflex-action spelling... well, it's not even worth a kopeck. It's just like being on a mechanical production line.'

Perekladin had held his tongue and even smiled submissively (the young man was the son of a State Councillor and was himself entitled

3

to a 10th-Class rank), but now, as he was going to bed, he was overcome by anger and indignation.

'I've been a civil servant for forty years,' he thought, 'and no one has ever called me a fool, and now look what kinds of critics have come out of the woodwork! 'Unconscious!'.. Lefrex-action! Mechanical production'..! Damn and blast it! It could be that I understand a good deal more than you, even if I haven't been to any of your universities!'

After mentally addressing his critic with all the curses he knew, and having warmed up under the blankets, Perekladin began to calm down.

'I do know… and I do understand…' he thought as he started to fall asleep. 'I know you shouldn't put a colon where a comma is needed, consequently I *am* aware, and I *do* understand what I am doing. Yes!.. So, young man… You need to live a little, and get some work experience, and then you can start judging your elders…'

A fiery comma flew like a meteor through the cluster of dark, smiling clouds in front of Perekladin's closed eyes as he dropped off to sleep. It was followed by a second and a third, and soon the endless dark background unfolding before his imagination was covered with dense clusters of flying commas…

'Take these commas for instance…' thought Perekladin, feeling the pleasurable sensation of his limbs going numb as sleep approached. 'I understand them very well… If you want I can find a place for each one of them… and… and I use them consciously too, not just willy-nilly. Test me and you'll see… Commas are placed in various places, where they are needed and where they are not needed. The more confusing a document turns out to be, the more commas you need. You place them in front of "in which case", and in front of "so that". And if you have to make a list of officials, then you need to separate each one with a comma… So I do know!'

The golden commas spun round and disappeared. Fiery full stops flew over to take their place…

'But the full stop is what you put at the end of a document… You also put one where you need to have a big breathing space and look at your audience. And you need a full stop after all the long bits, so the secretary's mouth won't be too dry when he is reading. You don't put a full stop anywhere else…'

The commas swooped down again… They mingled with the full stops, spun round and Perekladin now saw a whole host of semi-colons and colons…

'And I know about them too…' he thought. 'Where there aren't many commas and lots of full stops, that's where you need a semi-colon. I always put a semi-colon in front of "but" and "consequently"… Well, and what about colons? Colons come after phrases like "the following was resolved", "the following was decided"…'

The semi-colons and colons grew dim. A queue of question marks now lined up. They jumped out of the clouds and started doing the can-can…

'The question mark – I can deal with that! Even if there are a thousand of them, I'll find them all a place. You always use them when you need to make an enquiry, or if you have to inquire about a document… "Where has the remainder of the sum for such-and-such a year been transferred?", for example, or "Would it not be possible for the police authorities with regard to the said Ivanov etcetera etcetera..?"'

The question marks nodded their hooks approvingly and instantly stretched out into exclamation marks as if under command…

'Hmm!.. This punctuation mark is often used at the beginning of letters. As in "My dear sir!" or "Your excellency, dear father and benefactor!.." But what about in official papers?'

The exclamation marks grew even more elongated then stopped in expectation…

'You use them in official documents when… er… that is… what *is* the rule? Hmm! When do you actually use them in official documents then? Hang on… If I can just remember… Hmm!'

Perekladin opened his eyes and turned over on to his other side. But barely had he managed to close his eyes again when the exclamation marks reappeared against the dark background.

'Damn and blast… When do you need to use them?' he pondered, trying to drive the uninvited guests out of his imagination. 'Surely I haven't forgotten? Either I have forgotten or else… I have never actually used them…'

Perekladin started to recall the contents of all the documents he had written over the forty years in which he had been employed; but however hard he thought, however furrowed his brow became, he could not find a single instance of an exclamation mark in his past.

'Well I never did! I've been writing official documents for forty years and have not once used an exclamation mark... Hmm! But when the devil do you use them then?'

From behind the row of fiery exclamation marks appeared the snide laughing face of the young critic. The exclamation marks themselves grinned and then merged into one huge exclamation mark.

Perekladin shook his head and opened his eyes.

'Hell...' he thought. 'Tomorrow I've got to get up for church, and I can't get this devilry out of my head... Damn! When *do* you use an exclamation mark? So much for practice! So much for becoming a dab hand! Not one exclamation mark in forty years! Huh?'

Perekladin crossed himself and closed his eyes, but immediately opened them again: the big exclamation mark was still standing against the dark background...

'Damn! At this rate I'll never get to sleep.' 'Marfusha!' he called out to his wife, who often boasted about the fact that she had been to boarding school. 'You don't happen to know, my love, where you put exclamation marks in official papers do you?'

'Of course I do! I didn't spend seven years at boarding school for nothing. I remember all my grammar off by heart. You use them when you are addressing somebody, in exclamations, and in expressions of exaltation, indignation, joy, anger and other such feelings.'

'I see...' thought Perekladin. 'Exultation, indignation, joy, anger and other such feelings...'

The Collegiate Secretary started to think... He had been writing official papers for forty years, and had written thousands upon thousands of them, but he could not remember a single line which expressed exultation, indignation or anything like that...

'And other such feelings...' he thought. 'But when do you need feelings in official papers? Even someone without any feelings at all could write them...'

The face of the young critic again peeped out from behind the fiery exclamation mark and smirked at him. Perekladin got up and then went and sat down on the bed. His head hurt, and a cold sweat had broken out on his brow... The icon lamp was flickering gently in the corner, the furniture looked festive and clean, everything exuded a feeling of warmth and a woman's touch, but our poor official was feeling all cold and shivery, as if he had fallen ill with typhoid. The exclamation mark no longer stood before his closed eyes, but in front of him, in the room, near his wife's dressing table and it was winking slyly at him...

'Typewriter! Machine!' the apparition whispered, blowing a chilly coldness on to the official. 'Unfeeling lump of wood!'

The official wrapped himself up in the blankets, but he also saw the apparition underneath the blankets; he pressed his face into his wife's shoulder and it popped out from behind her shoulder too... Poor Perekladin was tormented all night long, but the apparition did not leave him the following day either. He saw it everywhere: in his boots when he was putting them on, in his cup of tea, in his St Stanislav[2] medal...

'And other such feelings....' he thought. 'I have never had any feelings, it's true... And now I've got to go to sign the Christmas card for the boss.... But is that something you do with feelings? It's no good... I am just a congratulatory machine...'

When Perekladin went out on to the street and hailed a cab, it seemed to him that an exclamation mark rolled up instead of a cab.

He walked into the lobby of his boss's office, and instead of the porter he saw the exclamation mark again... And all this filled him with exultation, indignation and anger... The pen also looked like an exclamation mark. Perekladin took it, dipped the pen in ink and signed:

'Collegiate Secretary Efim Perekladin!!!'

And as he inserted those three exclamation marks he experienced exultation, indignation, joy and burning rage.

'Take this! Take this!' he muttered, pressing hard with his pen.

The exclamation mark was satisfied and vanished.

The streets are a picture of hell in a golden frame. If it were not for the festive expression on the faces of doormen and policemen, you might have thought that the enemy had landed in the capital. Smart sleighs and carriages are dashing back and forth, creating noise and commotion... People are hurrying along the pavements to pay visits, their tongues hanging out, and their eyes rolling... They are scurrying past at such a rate that if Potiphar's wife was to grasp some Collegiate Registrar by the coat-tails, she would be left holding on to not just the coat-tails, but the civil servant's entire side, complete with liver and spleen...

Suddenly an ear-splitting police whistle can be heard. What has happened? The doormen leave their positions and run in the direction of the whistle...

'Move along now! Keep walking! Nothing for you to see here! Never seen a dead body, is that it? You people...'

A well-dressed man in a beaver fur coat and new rubber galoshes is stretched out on the pavement by one of the doorways... A pair of broken spectacles lies near his deathly pale, newly shaven face. The fur coat has come unbuttoned on his chest, and the assembled crowd can see a bit of his frock-coat and a St Stanislav medal, Third Class. His chest is moving up and down slowly and heavily, his eyes are shut...

'Sir!' says a policeman, poking the civil servant. 'Sir, it is not permitted to lie here! Your honour!'

But not a peep from the gentleman... Having fussed over him for about five minutes without managing to bring him round, the custodians of the law put him into a cab and take him to casualty...

'Nice trousers!' says the policeman while he helps the medical attendant to undress the sick man. 'Must have cost about six roubles. And that waistcoat is pretty smart too... To judge from his trousers, he's from the nobility...'

Having lain in casualty for about an hour and a half, and drunk a whole phial of valerian, the civil servant comes to... They find out that he is Titular Councillor Gerasim Kuzmich Sinkleteyev.

'Where does it hurt?' asks the police doctor.

'Happy New Year, Happy New Year...' he mumbles, staring blankly at the ceiling and breathing heavily.

'The same to you... But... where does it hurt? Why did you fall down? Try and remember! Was it something you drank?'

'Mmm... no...'

'So what made you feel so poorly?'

'I can't remember... I... I was doing the rounds...'

'So did you have lots of people to visit?'

'No, not really... just a few... I came home from church... had a cup of tea, then I set off for Nikolay Mikhailich's... I had to sign the card there, of course... From there I went down Ofitserskaya Street to Kachalkin's... I had to sign the card there too... And I also remember that there was a draught blowing in the hall there... From Kachalkin's I crossed to the Vyborg Side and dropped by Ivan Ivanych's... Signed there...'

'Another civil servant has been brought in!' announces the policeman.

'From Ivan Ivanych's,' Sinkleteyev continues, 'I went to shake hands with Khrymov the merchant... I dropped in to wish his family a Happy New Year... They suggested we raise a glass... And how could I refuse? You offend people if you refuse... So, I downed about three glasses... ate a bit of sausage... And from there I went across to the Petersburg Side to pay a call on Likhodeyev... He is a good man...'

'You did all of this on foot?'

'Yes, on foot... I signed the card at Likhodeyev's... From there I went to Pelageya Emelyanovna's... Who sat me down to breakfast and treated me to coffee. The coffee made me break out in a sweat – it must have gone to my head... From Pelageya Emelyanovna I went to Obleukhov... Vasily Obleukhov he's called, it was his name day... So I couldn't upset him by refusing a piece of name day cake...'

'A retired officer and two civil servants have been brought in!' reports the policeman.

'I had a piece of cake, a shot of rowanberry liqueur and went on to Sadovaya Street to visit Izyumov... At Izyumov's I had a cold beer... that hit the spot... From Izyumov I went to Koshkin, and then to Karl Karlich... and from there to my uncle, Pyotr Semyonich... His niece Nastya gave me some hot chocolate to drink… Then I dropped in on Lyapkin… No, I tell a lie, it wasn't Lapkin, it was Darya Nikodimovna… I went to Lyapkin after visiting her… Anyway, I felt fine all the time… Then I visited Ivanov, Kurdyukov and Shiller, and I also visited Colonel Poroshkov, and I felt fine there too… I visited Dunkin the merchant… He insisted I had a glass of cognac and ate some sausage and cabbage… I had about three glasses… and I ate a couple of sausages, but I still felt alright… It was only when I was leaving Ryzhov's that I felt my head… beginning to spin… I started to feel weak… I don't know why…'

'You have worn yourself out… Have a little rest, and we will send you home…'

'I can't go home…' groans Sinkleteyev. 'I still have to call on my brother-in-law Kuzma Vavilich… the executor, and Natalya Egorovna… There are a lot of people I still haven't visited…'

'And you shouldn't be visiting them either.'

'I have to… You've got to wish people a Happy New Year… It's important… My life won't be worth living if I don't call on Natalya Egorovna… You are going to have to discharge me doctor, you must…'

Sinkleteyev stands up and reaches for his clothes.

'You can go home if you want,' says the doctor, 'but you shouldn't even think about paying any more visits…'

'Oh, it will be alright…' says Sinkleteyev with a sigh. 'I'll take it easy…'

The civil servant gets dressed slowly, wraps himself up in his fur coat and totters unsteadily out on to the street.

'Five more civil servants have been brought in!' announces the policeman. 'Where shall I put them?'

COMPETITION

The editors of *Fragments* announce a competition with *a prize to be awarded*.

Whoever writes *the best love letter* will win: a photograph of a pretty woman, a document (signed by the editor and the competition judges) certifying that on such-and-such a date, so-and-so won this competition, and with it a free subscription for the coming year, or any year in the future, at his choosing. The prize-winning letter, moreover, will be printed in *Fragments*, and the author will receive 15 kopecks a line.

Competition rules: 1) Competition entrants may only be of the male gender. 2) The letter must be sent to the editorial office of *Fragments* no later than 1st March of this year and accompanied by the surname and address of the author. 3) The author must declare his love in the letter; prove that he is really in love and is suffering; draw a contrast between common or garden enthusiasm and real love; describe his new feelings without going into deep analysis; propose marriage; express jealousy of X and Y; describe the torments he experiences at the mere thought of being refused; pay his respects to her Papa and Mama; carefully and subtly enquire about the dowry and... none of this can exceed fifty lines. 4) Conditio sine qua non: the author must be literary, decorous, tender, playful and poetic. Whining, fake classicism and bad verse is not allowed. That's it.

The judges will be *ladies*.

Ilya Sergeyich Peplov and his wife Kleopatra Petrovna were standing by the door and listening out eagerly. Behind the door a declaration of love was clearly taking place in the little room; it was a declaration of love involving their daughter Natashenka, and Shchupkin the district school teacher.

'He's biting!' whispered Peplov, quivering with impatience and rubbing his hands together. 'So look, Petrovna, as soon as they start talking about feelings, you must straight away take the icon down from the wall and we'll go in and bless them… We'll have them in the net… A blessing with the icon is sacred and can't be undone… There's no getting out of it then; even if you went to court you'd be hard pushed to undo it.'

But this was the conversation going on behind the door:

'Let's leave your character out of it!' said Shchupkin as he struck a match on his checked trousers. 'I didn't write you any letters!'

'Oh, sure! As if I don't know your handwriting!' laughed the girl, simpering in an affected way, and every now and then glancing at herself in the mirror. 'I recognised it immediately! You are all so weird! Here you are, a calligraphy teacher, and your writing looks like the scratchings of a hen! How can you teach writing when you write so badly yourself?'

'Hmm!.. That does not mean anything. In calligraphy it's not the handwriting which is important; the main thing is that the pupils do not doze off. You have to rap them on the head with the ruler, or on the knee… Handwriting is neither here nor there! A waste of time! Nekrasov was a writer, and it's shameful to see how he wrote. They show his handwriting in his Collected Works.'

'You are hardly comparable to Nekrasov… (sigh). I'd gladly marry a writer. He would always be writing poems and dedicating them to me!'

'I can write you poems if you wish.'

'What can you write about then?'

'About love… about feelings… about your eyes… Just wait till you read them – you will go mad… You will shed tears! So if I write you poetic verses, will you let me kiss your hand?'

'No need to stand on ceremony!... You can kiss it right now!'

Shchupkin jumped up, goggle-eyed, and pounced on the puffy little hand which smelled of soap.

'Take the icon down!' said Peplov, elbowing his wife in his haste to do up his buttons, and turning pale with excitement. 'Come on, let's go in!'

And without a second's delay, Peplov flung open the door.

'Children...' he started to mumble, raising his hands and blinking with teary eyes. 'The Lord blesses you, my children... Live... be fruitful... multiply...'

'And... and I bless you too...' said Mama, crying with happiness. 'I wish you much happiness, my dears! Oh, you're taking away my only treasure!' she said, turning to Shchupkin. 'You must love my daughter, and take care of her...'

Shchupkin's jaw dropped in amazement and fright. The parents' assault was so bold and sudden that he could not utter a single word.

'Now I've had it! They've got me!' he thought, overcome with horror. 'I'm done for now! No escaping!'

And he hung his head, as if wanting to say: 'Take me, I'm conquered!'

'I give you... my blessing,' Papa continued, also starting to cry. 'Natashenka, my dear daughter... Stand by his side... Petrovna, give me the icon...'

But suddenly Papa stopped crying, and his face became twisted with rage.

'You cretin!' he said angrily to his wife. 'Is this an icon?'

'Oh Lord in heaven!'

What happened? The calligraphy teacher raised his eyes timidly and saw that he was saved: in her haste, Mama had taken a portrait of the writer Lazhechnikov down from the wall instead of the icon. Old Peplov and his wife Kleopatra Petrovna stood in embarrassment, not knowing what to say or do. The calligraphy teacher took advantage of their embarrassment and fled.

'How can I help you?' asks a female voice.

'Put me through to the Slavyansky Bazaar restaurant please.'[3]

'Certainly!'

Within three minutes I hear a ring… I clasp the receiver to my ear and hear sounds of an indeterminate character: a bit like the wind blowing, or peas being sprinkled… Someone is murmuring something…

'Are any of your private rooms available?' I ask.

'There's no one at home…' answers a child's hesitant voice. 'Papa and Mama have gone to Serafima Petrovna's, and Louisa Frantsovna has got the flu.'

'Who are you? Are you from the Slavyansky Bazaar?'

'I'm Seryozha… My Papa is a doctor… He sees patients in the morning…'

'Dear boy, I don't need a doctor, but the Slavyansky Bazaar…'

'What bazaar? (laughter). Now I know who you are… You're Pavel Andreyich… We got a letter from Katya! (laughter). She is getting married to an officer… So when are you going to buy me some paints?'

I go away from the telephone and ring up again about ten minutes later.

'Put me through to the Slavyansky Bazaar!' I request.

'At last!' answers a hoarse bass. 'Is Fuchs with you?'

'What Fuchs are you talking about? I want to be connected to the Slavyansky Bazaar!!'

'You are in the Slavyansky Bazaar are you? Alright, I'll come over… And we'll finish our business today… I'll be on my way… Order me a portion of sturgeon soup, dear boy… I haven't had lunch yet…'

'Confound it! What a business!' I think, going away from the telephone. 'Maybe I don't know how to use a telephone, and just keep getting it wrong… So, how does it go? First you have to turn this little thing, then lift this thing and put it to your ear… And then what? Then you have to hang this thing on these little things and turn this little thing three times… I think that's right!'

I ring again. No answer. Then I ring in such agitation that there is a danger I will actually break the telephone. In the earpiece I can hear a noise which sounds like mice running across a piece of paper…

'Who am I talking to?' I shout. 'Answer! Speak louder!'

'Timofey Vaksin and Sons, Manufacturers…'

'I most humbly thank you… But your Manufacturers are not what I am after…'

'Is that Sychov? The calico has already been sent over to you…'

I hang up the earpiece and again begin to question whether I have got something wrong or not. I read through the 'regulations', smoke a cigarette and ring again. No answer…

'The telephone at the Slavyansky Bazaar must be faulty,' I think. 'I'll try and speak to the Hermitage instead.'

I study the section of the regulations dealing with how to talk to the central exchange, and make my call…

'Put me through to the Hermitage restaurant!' I shout. 'the Her-mi-tage!!'

Five minutes go by, then ten… My patience begins to wear out, but then suddenly – hurray! – the telephone rings.

'Who am I talking to?' I ask.

'Central exchange…'

'Confound it! Put me through to the Hermitage! I beg you!'

'Was that Ferrein the Chemist?'

'The Her-mi-tage!!'

'Very good…'

'So, it looks like my torment is over…' I think. 'Goodness me, I'm sweating!'

The telephone rings. I grab the earpiece and enquire:

'Do you have any private rooms?'

'Papa and Mama have gone to Serafima Petrovna's, and Louisa Frantsovna has the flu… There's no one at home!'

'Is that you, Seryozha?'

'Yes… Who's that? (laughter)… Pavel Andreyich? Why didn't you come round yesterday? (laughter). Papa showed Chinese shadows… He put on Mama's hat and pretended to be Avdotya Nikolaevna…'

Seryozha's voice suddenly breaks off and silence follows. I hang up the earpiece and dial for the next three minutes, until my fingers start aching.

'Put me through to the Hermitage!' I shout. 'The restaurant on Trubnaya Square! Can you hear me or not?'

'I can hear you perfectly well, sir... But this is the Slavyansky Bazaar, not the Hermitage.'

'I'm talking to the Slavyansky Bazaar?'

'That's correct... the Slavyansky Bazaar.'

'Confound it! I don't understand anything! Do you have any private rooms?'

'I'll just find out, sir.'

A minute goes by, then another... A light vocal tremor runs down the earpiece ... I listen and do not understand anything...

'Please answer me: do you have any private rooms?'

'What is it you need?' asks a female voice.

'Are you from the Slavyansky Bazaar?'

'Central exchange...'

(continuation to the *nec plus ultra*)

KIDS

Papa, Mama and Auntie Nadia are not at home. They have gone to a christening at the house of the old officer who rides a little grey horse. Grisha, Anya, Alyosha, Sonya, and the cook's son Andrey are all sitting round the table in the dining room playing lotto while they wait for them to come back. To be honest, it is past their bedtime, but they can hardly be expected to go to sleep before they have found out from Mama what the baby being christened was like, and what food they were given for supper, can they? The table, lit by a lamp hanging from the ceiling, is covered with a bright array of numbers, nutshells, pieces of paper and glass counters. In front of each player are two cards and a heap of counters for covering up the numbers. In the middle of the table is a little white dish containing five-kopeck pieces. Near the dish is a half-eaten apple, a pair of scissors, and a plate in which they are supposed to put the nutshells. The children are playing for money: the stake is a kopeck. The rules are that anyone who cheats is immediately out of the game. There is no one else in the dining room. Agafya Ivanovna the nanny is sitting downstairs in the kitchen, teaching the cook to cut fabric, while Vasya, the eldest brother, a pupil in the fifth form, is moping on the couch in the drawing room.

They are passionately absorbed in the game. Grisha's face betrays the greatest absorption. He is a small, nine-year-old boy with a shaved head, chubby cheeks, and thick lips like a negro. Since he is already in the preparatory class, he is regarded as grown-up, and the cleverest of them. He only ever plays for money. If there had been no kopecks in the dish, he would long ago have been asleep. His brown eyes roam restlessly and jealously over the cards of his partners. Fear that he may not win, envy, and the financial calculations filling his shaven head are preventing him from sitting still and concentrating. He is fidgeting about like a monkey. When he wins, he grabs the money greedily, and immediately stashes it away in his pocket. His sister Anya, an eight year old with a pointed chin, and clever, bright eyes, is also afraid of someone else winning. She watches the other players like a hawk, her face alternately flushing and going pale. She is not interested in the kopecks. For her, enjoying the game is a question of self-esteem. The other sister, Sonya, a girl of six, with a mop of curly hair and the kind of complexion only to be found among very healthy children, expensive dolls and tins of sweets, is playing lotto just for the sake of playing. Her face is a picture of rapt emotion, and she laughs and claps her hands no matter who wins each round. Alyosha, a roly-poly, tubby little lad, sits there huffing and puffing, his eyes fixed on the cards. There is nothing mercenary or vain about him. He is just happy that he is not being banished from the table and taken to bed. He might look placid, but he is a real rascal underneath. He sat down not so much for the lotto but for all the disagreements which inevitably arise during games. He loves it when someone gets hit or is called names. He has been needing to visit a particular place for a long time now, but he cannot get up from the table even for a minute, because he is scared his counters and kopecks might be swiped while he is gone. Since he only knows the primary numbers and those numbers ending in nought, Anya places the counters for him. The fifth partner, Andrey, the cook's son, an unhealthy-looking, swarthy boy in a calico shirt, with a little bronze cross on his chest, stands motionless, looking dreamily at the numbers. He does not care about winning money, or about other people doing better than him, because he is completely engrossed in the arithmetics of the game, and in its simple philosophy: there are so many numbers in the world, and goodness knows how they manage not to get muddled up!

Apart from Sonya and Alyosha, they all take it in turns to shout out the numbers. Since the numbers themselves are quite boring, they have developed a system of funny nicknames and descriptions. So seven is called the poker, eleven is chopsticks, seventy-seven is Sevastian Seviastianich, ninety is grandfather, and so on. The game is very lively.

'Thirty-two!' shouts Grisha, pulling the little yellow balls out of his father's hat. 'Seventeen! The poker! Twenty-eight – shut the gate!'

Anya can see that Andrey has missed twenty-eight on his card. Another time she would have pointed it out to him, but since her self-esteem is sitting there on the dish together with her kopeck, she wants to win now.

'Twenty-three!' continues Grisha. 'Sevastian Seviastianich! Nine!'

'Look, a cockroach!' shrieks Sonya, pointing to the cockroach scuttling across the table. 'Aagh!'

'Don't kill him,' says Alyosha in his bass voice. 'Maybe he has children…'

Sonya follows the cockroach with her eyes, and wonders about his children: he must have lots of little cockroach babies!

'Forty-three! One!' continues Grisha, worrying that Anya has already covered up two lots of squares. 'Six!'

'Full house! I've won!' shouts Sonya, rolling her eyes coyly, and chortling with glee.

Her partners pull long faces.

'Not until we've checked!' says Grisha, looking at Sonya with hatred.

As the oldest and cleverest of them, Grisha has decided he should be the judge. Whatever he wants, they go along with. After spending a long time painstakingly checking Sonya's card, it turns out, to the great regret of her partners, that she has not cheated. The next round starts.

'Guess what I saw yesterday!' says Anya as if to herself. 'Filipp Filippich sort of turned back his eyelids, and his eyes went all red and scary like he was an evil spirit.'

'I saw him doing that too,' says Grisha. 'Eight! Well, at our school there is a boy who can wiggle his ears. Twenty-seven!'

Andrey raises his eyes to look at Grisha, thinks for a while, then says:

'I can wiggle my ears too…'

'Go on then, show us!'

Andrey wiggles his eyes, his lips and his fingers, and he thinks his ears have started wiggling too. General laughter.

'He's horrid, that Filipp Filippich,' says Sonya with a sigh. 'Yesterday he came into the nursery when I was still in my nightgown…. It felt quite indecent!'

'Full house!' shouts out Grisha suddenly, grabbing the money in the dish. 'I've won! You can check if you want!'

The cook's son raises his eyes and turns pale.

'That means I can't play any more,' he whispers.

'Why?'

'Because… because I don't have any more money.'

19

'You can't play without money!' says Grisha.

Andrey roots around in his pockets one last time. When he does not find anything except crumbs and a chewed pencil stub, the corners of his mouth turn down, and he starts blinking furiously. He is about to start crying…

'I'll put some money in for you!' says Sonya, unable to bear his pained look. 'But you've got to pay me back later.'

The money is doled out, and the game continues.

'I think I can hear a bell ringing,' says Anya, his eyes widening.

They all stop playing and stare through the dark window, open-mouthed. The reflection of the lamp flickers beyond the darkness.

'I heard that.'

'They only ring bells at night in the cemetery…' says Andrey.

'Why do they ring them there?'

'So robbers don't get into the church. They are afraid of the bell-ringing.'

'But why would robbers want to get into the church?' Sonya asks.

'It's obvious – to kill the watchmen!'

A minute goes by in silence. They all look at each other, shudder, then go on playing. This time Andrey wins.

'He cheated,' says Alyosha in his bass voice without any reason.

'You're lying, I didn't cheat!'

Andrey goes pale, twists his mouth, and thwacks Alyosha on the head! Alyosha glowers, then jumps up, and with one knee on the table, slaps Andrey on the cheek! They both slap each other again and start howling. Sonya also starts crying because she cannot bear such terrible scenes, and the dining room is filled with the deafening noise of many children bawling at once. But do not think that this means the end of the game. Within five minutes the children are chattering happily and laughing again. Their faces are tear-stained, but that does not stop them from smiling. Alyosha is actually happy, because there was an argument!

The fifth-form pupil Vasya comes into the dining room. His sleepy face wears an expression of dismay.

'This is outrageous!' he thinks, seeing Grisha feeling the pocket in which his kopecks are jingling. 'Surely children shouldn't be given money! And surely they shouldn't be gambling either! So much for education. It's outrageous!'

But the children play so well that he soon wants to join in and try his luck.

'Wait a second, I want to sit down and play,' he says.

'Put in a kopeck then!'

'Hang on,' he says, rummaging in his pockets. 'Look, I don't have a kopeck, but here's a rouble. I'll put a rouble in.'

'No, no, no… you've got to put in a kopeck!'

'You're a bunch of idiots. A rouble is worth more than a kopeck,' says the high school student. 'Whoever wins can pay me back.'

'No, thanks! You can go away!'

The fifth-form pupil shrugs his shoulders and goes into the kitchen to borrow some change from the servants. But there are no kopecks in the kitchen either.

'In that case, how about you give me some change,' he pesters Grisha, as he comes out of the kitchen. 'I'll give you something in return. You don't want to? Well, sell me ten kopecks for a rouble then.'

Grisha looks suspiciously at Vasya out of the corner of his eye. Is this some kind of dirty trick, or a swindle?

'I don't want to,' he says, holding on to his pocket.

Vasya begins to lose his temper, and curses, calling the players blockheads and imbeciles.

'Alright, I'll put money in for you, Vasya!' says Sonya. 'Sit down!'

The schoolboy sits down and puts two cards in front of him. Anya begins to read out the numbers.

'I've dropped a kopeck!' declares Grisha suddenly in a worried voice. 'Wait!'

They pick up a lamp and crawl underneath the table to look for the kopeck. Their hands come across nutshells and spittle, and their heads bang together, but they do not find the kopeck. They start looking again, and carry on looking until Vasya snatches the lamp from Grisha and puts it back in its place. Grisha goes on looking in the darkness.

But finally the kopeck is found. The players sit down at the table with the intention of continuing with the game.

'Sonya is asleep!' Alyosha declares.

Having rested her curly head on her arms, Sonya is slumbering soundly, as if she had dropped off to sleep an hour ago. She just happened to fall asleep while the others were looking for the kopeck.

'Go and lie down on Mama's bed!' says Anya, taking her out of the dining room. 'Go on!'

They all troop off to escort her, and in about five minutes Mama's bed presents a curious spectacle. Sonya is asleep. Near her Alyosha is snoring. Grisha and Anya have rested their heads on Sonya and Alyosha's legs, and they are also asleep. The cook's son Andrey has managed to squeeze in too. Near them are scattered the kopecks, which have lost their power until the next game. Good night!

GRIEF

Whom to tell of my sadness?... [4]

Evening twilight. Large flakes of wet snow are lazily circling the street-lamps which have just been lit, and settling in a soft, thin layer on roofs, the backs of horses, shoulders and hats. Iona Potapov the cabby is all white, like a ghost. He is as hunched up as a living person can be, and sitting in his sleigh without moving a muscle. He probably would not consider it worth shaking the snow off himself even if a whole snowdrift fell on him... His old mare is also white and motionless. Standing there stock-still, with her angular frame and legs as straight as sticks, she looks like one of those one-kopeck gingerbread horses close up. She is probably deep in thought. Having been torn away from the plough, from familiar grey scenes, and thrown into this maelstrom of monstrous lights, with its relentless din and people rushing about, it would be impossible not to think...

Iona and his little horse have not moved for a long time now. They left the yard before lunch even, and they have yet to take a fare. And now the evening dusk is descending on the city. The pallor of the streetlamps gives way to bright colours, and the bustle on the street gets noisier.

'Cabby, to the Vyborg Side!' Iona hears. 'Cabby!'

Iona gives a shudder, and through his eyelashes, which are coated with snow, sees an officer in a greatcoat and hood.

'To the Vyborg Side!' the officer repeats. 'Are you asleep or something? To the Vyborg Side!'

Iona jerks the reins in a gesture of assent, which causes whole layers of snow to fall off his shoulders and off his horse's back... The officer gets into the sleigh. The cabby makes a clicking sound, stretches out his neck like a swan, sits up, and brandishes his whip, from habit rather than need, it has to be said. The little horse also stretches out her neck, bends her stick-like legs and moves forward hesitantly...

'Where do you think you are going, you old goblin?' At first Iona hears cries from the dark mass of people walking up and down the street. 'Where the hell are you heading? Keep to the right!'

'You can't even drive! Keep to the right!' exclaims the officer angrily.

A coachman curses him from his carriage, and a pedestrian fumes and shakes the snow off his sleeve, his shoulder having collided with the horse's muzzle while he was running across the road. Iona fidgets on his box, as if sitting on needles; he sticks his elbows out and rolls his eyes like a madman, as if he does not understand where he is, or why he is there.

'What a bunch of scoundrels!' jokes the officer. 'They seem to be doing their best either to bump into you or end up in the horse's path. I'm sure it's on purpose.'

Iona looks round at his fare and moves his lips... He obviously wants to say something, but nothing except a croak comes out of his throat.

'What?' asks the officer.

Iona twists his mouth into a smile, strains his throat and wheezes:

'You know, sir, my... er, son died this week.'

'Hmm!.. What did he die of?'

Iona turns right round to face his fare and says:

'Wish I knew! Must have been from fever... He was in hospital for three days and then he passed away... God's will.'

'Get the devil out of the way!' comes a voice booming out of the darkness. 'Taking the scenic route, are you, you old cur? Use your eyes!'

'Come on, get a move on...' says his passenger. 'We'll be here till morning at this rate. Get cracking!'

The cabby stretches his neck out again, sits up straight, and waves his whip with a heavy grace. He looks round a few times at his fare afterwards, but the latter has closed his eyes and is obviously not in the mood for listening. Having deposited him on the Vyborg Side, he pulls up next to a tavern, huddles up again on his box and does not budge... Once more wet snow whitewashes him and his horse. A hour passes, then another...

Three young men in the middle of a slanging match are walking along the pavement, scuffing their galoshes noisily: two of them are tall and thin like beanpoles; the third is small and hunch-backed.

'Cabby, to the Police Bridge!' shouts the hunchback in a rasping voice. 'There's three of us... twenty kopecks!'

Iona pulls on the reins and clicks his tongue. Twenty kopecks is not a fair price, but that's the least of his worries… A rouble or five kopecks – it's all the same to him now, just as long as he has some passengers… Jostling each other and cursing, the young men come up to the sleigh, and then all three try and squash on to the seat at the same time. They start discussing which two will get to sit down, and who will have to stand. After much wrangling, sulking and exchanges of insults, they decide that the hunchback should stand, since he is the smallest.

'Right, get a move on!' rasps the hunchback, breathing down Iona's neck as he steadies himself. 'Crack that whip! Hey, old codger, that hat you're wearing – must be the worst in Petersburg!..'

'Hee-hee… Hee-hee…' chuckles Iona. 'It's all I've got…'

'Well, you get a move on it's all I've got! Are you going to go at this speed all the way? And what would you say to a thwack on the neck?..'

'I've got a splitting headache…' says one of the beanpoles. 'Vaska and I drank four bottles of brandy last night at Dukmasovs'.'

'Why do you have to lie?' the other beanpole reacts angrily. 'He's lying through his teeth.'

'I swear to God, it's the truth…'

'Sure, and have you heard the one about the louse which coughed?'

'Hee-hee,' sniggers Iona. 'You gentlemen are a real laugh!'

'To hell with you!' retorts the hunchback in irritation. 'Are you going to get a move on or not, you old slacker? We're hardly moving. Give her a crack of your whip! Come on, damn you! Give it to her!'

Behind his back Iona can feel the twisting body of the hunchback and the vibrations of his voice. He hears the swearing addressed to him, sees people, and little by little the feeling of loneliness begins to be lifted from his heart. The hunchback carries on swearing until he chokes on a particularly elaborate and prolonged piece of cursing, and is stopped by a coughing fit. The beanpoles start talking about some Nadezhda Petrovna or other. Iona looks round at them. After waiting for a brief pause in the conversation, he looks round again and murmurs:

'You know, this week… my, er, son died!'

'We'll all die…' says the hunchback with a sigh, wiping his lips after all his coughing. 'Come on, get a move on! I really can't put up with this any longer, gentlemen! When on earth is he going to get us there?'

'Well, you perk him up a bit... Give it to him in the neck!'

'Do you hear, you decrepit old fool? I'm going to thump you in the neck!.. One may as well walk, standing on ceremony with the likes of you!.. You vile creature, do you hear? Or don't you give a damn about what we say?'

And Iona hears rather than feels the sound of the thud on his neck.

'Hee-hee...' he laughs. 'You gentlemen are a laugh... Good health to you!'

'Hey, cabby, are you married?' asks one of the beanpoles.

'Me, married? Hee-hee... you gentlemen are a right laugh! I've only got one wife now, and that's the damp earth... Ho-ho-ho... The grave, I mean! My son's gone and died, but I'm still alive... It's all a bit odd, because death knocked on the wrong door... Should have come for me, but went to my son instead...'

And Iona turns round so he can tell them how his son died, but just then the hunchback heaves a sigh of relief, and declares that they have finally arrived, thank goodness. After receiving his twenty kopecks, Iona spends a long time watching the revellers disappearing through a dark doorway. He is on his own again, and silence once again surrounds him... The grief which had gone for a short while comes back again and wrenches at his heart with even greater force. In his agony, Iona's eyes anxiously scan the crowds pouring down both sides of the street: is there not one person out of those thousands who might listen to him? But the crowds throng past, noticing neither him nor his grief... His grief is immense and boundless. If you were to open up Iona's chest and pour all the grief out of it, you would probably flood the entire planet, yet it is not visible. It has managed to squeeze into such a minute receptacle that you would not be able to see it in brightest daylight.

Iona sees a doorman with a sack and decides to talk to him.

'Have you got the time, my friend?' he asks.

'Past nine... What are you hanging about here for? Be off with you!'

Iona moves a few feet away, then doubles over and gives in to his grief... Trying to talk to people, he realises now, is pointless. But five minutes have barely gone by when he sits up, shakes his head as if in acute pain, and tugs on the reins... He can't bear it any more.

'To the yard!' he thinks. 'Back to the yard!'

And the little horse breaks into a trot as if reading his mind. About an hour and a half later, Iona is already sitting by the big dirty stove. There are people snoring on the stove, on the floor and on the benches. The air is foul-smelling and stuffy... Iona takes one look at the people sleeping, scratches himself and regrets coming home so early...

'And I haven't even earned enough to pay for the oats,' he thinks. 'No wonder I'm full of grief. A man who knows his job... who isn't hungry, and whose horse isn't hungry, will always feel alright.'

In one corner a young cabby sits up, grunts sleepily, and stretches out for the bucket of water.

'You thirsty, then?' asks Iona.

'That's why I am having a drink!'

'I see... Well, cheers... You know, mate, my son died... Did you hear? In the hospital this week. What a business!'

Iona looks to see what effect his words are having, but sees nothing. The young man has covered his head and is already asleep. The old man sighs and scratches himself... The young fellow wanted to drink, and he wants to talk. It will soon be a week since his son has died, and he still has not managed to talk to anyone about it properly... He needs to have a decent talk with someone, and not be rushed... He needs to tell the story of how his son fell ill, how he suffered, what his last words were, and how he died... And he has to describe the funeral, and the trip to the hospital to collect his son's clothes. His daughter Anisya is left in the village... So he needs to talk about her too... There's a lot for him to talk about just now. And he needs a listener who will sigh, and grieve, and lament... And it would be even better to talk to a woman. They might be fools, but you only have to say two words and they start howling.

'I should go and have a look at the horse,' thinks Iona. 'I can always catch up on sleep later... No worries about that...'

He gets dressed and goes over to the stables where he keeps his horse. He is thinking about oats, and hay, and the weather... He cannot think about his son when he is alone... He could talk to someone else about him, but thinking about him on his own, and picturing him in his mind is unbearably painful...

'Are you chewing?' Iona asks his horse, seeing her shining eyes.

'Keep chewing then, keep chewing… If we don't earn enough for oats, we'll have to eat hay… Yes… I've got too old to be a cabby… It should be my son going out to work, you know, not me… He was a proper cabby, he was…'

Iona is silent for a while, and then continues:

'So that's how it is, old girl… Kuzma Ionych is no more… He has departed this life… He's gone and died, and what a waste. Now let's say you had a little foal, and you were its mother… And what if your little foal were to depart this life… You'd be sad, wouldn't you?'

The little horse chews, listens, and breathes on the hands of her master…

Iona gets carried away and tells her everything…

CONVERSATION BETWEEN A DRUNKARD
AND A SOBER DEVIL

Retired Collegiate Secretary Lakhmatov,[5] a former civil servant at the quartermaster's office, was sitting at home in his dining room, and thinking about brotherhood, equality and liberty as he downed his sixteenth glass. All of a sudden, a devil peeped out at him from behind the lamp… Lady readers, do not take fright. Do you know what a devil looks like? We are talking about a young man of pleasant appearance, with a face as black as tar, and with expressive red eyes… He has little horns on his head, even though he is not married… Fashionable centre parting with curls on each side, just like the French singer Capoul.[6] Body covered with green fur, whiffing of dog. Tail hanging down at the bottom of the back, ending in an arrow… Claws instead of fingers, horse's hooves instead of feet. Lakhmatov felt a bit awkward when he saw the devil, but when he remembered that green devils have the idiotic habit of appearing before anyone who is a bit drunk, he soon calmed down.

'With whom do I have the honour of speaking?' he enquired of his uninvited guest.

The devil became embarrassed and lowered his gaze.

'Don't be shy,' continued Lakhmatov. 'Come closer… I am a person without prejudice, and you can talk to me openly… from the heart… Who are you?'

The devil approached Lakhmatov hesitantly, tucked his tail in, and bowed politely.

'I am a devil, or a demon…' he said, introducing himself. 'I am employed as a civil servant in the special task force of his excellency, the director of the chancellery of hell, Mr Satan!'

'Oh yes, I've heard of that… Pleased to meet you. Have a seat! Would you like a vodka? You're most welcome… And what do you do?'

The devil became even more embarrassed…

'Strictly speaking, I don't have any specific occupation,' he replied, coughing in discomfort, and blowing his nose into the puzzle journal *Rebus*. 'It is true that we used to have an occupation… We used to tempt people… We would lead them astray from the path of goodness and lure them on to the way of evil… But that occupation, *entre nous soit dit*, is hardly worth the trouble nowadays… There isn't a path of goodness any more, so there is nothing to lead people astray from. And besides, people have become craftier than us… You try and tempt a person who has studied everything at university, and gone through fire and brimstone! How can I teach you to steal a rouble, when you have made off with thousands without any help from me?'

'That's all true… But surely you must do something?'

'Oh yes… Our previous job is purely symbolic now, but we do still have work… We tempt top-class ladies, goad youths into writing poetry, and make drunk merchants break mirrors… We stopped having any involvement in politics, literature, and the academic world a long time ago… We don't understand a jot of any of that… Many of us contribute to *Rebus*, and there are even some who have left hell and joined humanity… These retired devils who have joined humanity have married rich merchant women, and now live exceedingly well. Some of them practise law, others publish newspapers, and they are generally very active and respected people!'

'Excuse me asking, but what is your salary?'

'Our situation is the same as before…' replied the devil. 'The general package hasn't changed at all… As before, you get an apartment, with heating and electricity thrown in… We don't receive wages, because we are all considered supernumerary, and because being a devil is an honorary position… Generally speaking, it's a tough life to be honest, whatever you might think… It's a good thing people have taught us to take bribes, otherwise we'd have been done for long ago… We live on whatever we can procure… You supply sinners with provisions, and then, well… you nab them… Satan has grown old, spends his time going to the ballet to watch Virginia Zucchi, and can't be bothered with accounts now…'

Lakhmatov poured the devil a glass of vodka. Having downed it, the devil warmed to his theme. He revealed all the secrets of hell, poured out his soul, started crying, and seemed so likeable that Lakhmatov even let him stay the night. The devil slept in the stove and was delirious all night. By morning he had disappeared.

THE REQUIEM

In the Church of the Mother of God Who Shows the Way, in the village of Verkhnye Zaprudy, the Liturgy has just come to an end. The congregation has begun to stir itself, and is shuffling slowly out of the church. The only person not moving is the shopkeeper Andrey Andreyich, long-term resident intellectual of Verkhnye Zaprudy. He is standing by the right-hand choir platform, with his elbow resting on the rail, waiting. His clean-shaven, pudgy face, scarred from an earlier rash of spots, on this occasion bears two contrasting feelings: humility before the mysteries of our destiny, and boundless contempt for the long peasant coats and brightly coloured scarves passing by him. Because it is Sunday he is dressed to the nines. He is wearing a cloth coat with yellow bone buttons, long blue trousers not tucked in, and stout galoshes – the kind of huge, clodhopping galoshes only to be found on the feet of confident, sensible people of firm religious convictions.

His protuberant, sluggish eyes are trained on the iconostasis. He sees the long familiar faces of the saints, Matvey the warden puffing up his cheeks to blow out the candles, the darkened candlesticks, the worn carpet, Lopukhov the deacon beetling out from the sanctuary to take the communion bread to the churchwarden… All this he has seen a million times before, and knows as well as the five fingers on his hand… But there is, however, one thing that is a bit odd and not quite normal: Father Grigory is standing by the north door, still in his vestments, twitching his bushy eyebrows angrily.

'Who in heaven's name is he winking at?' the shopkeeper wonders. 'Hmm, he's started wagging his finger too! Good gracious, now he's stamping his foot as well… Holy Mother of God, whatever is going on? Whose attention is he trying to get?'

Andrey Andreyich looks round and sees that the church is by now completely deserted. There are about ten people clustered by the door, but they all have their back to the altar.

He hears the angry voice of Father Grigory. 'Come when you are called! What are you doing, standing there like a statue? It's you I am talking to!'

The shopkeeper looks at the irate red face of Father Grigory and only now realises that all the eyebrow-twitching and finger-waving may have been directed at him. He gives a start, moves away from the choir platform, and walks hesitantly in his noisy galoshes over towards the altar.

'Andrey Andreyich, was it you who put in a request during the liturgy for a prayer to be said for the eternal rest of Maria?' the priest asks, fixing his eyes angrily on his pudgy, perspiring face.[7]

'It was indeed.'

'Ah, so it was you then? You wrote it?'

And Father Grigory brandishes his note angrily in front of his eyes. On this slip, which Andrey Andreyich had handed in with the communion bread, was written in large wobbly letters: 'For the eternal rest of God's servant, the whore Maria.'

'Yes, Father, I did indeed write that.'

'How could you dare write such a thing?' hisses the priest in a protracted and hoarse whisper, full of rage and fear.

The shopkeeper looks at him in complete surprise and bewilderment, and himself takes fright: Father Grigory has never spoken in such a tone to Verkhnye Zaprudy intellectuals before! They are both silent for a moment as they meet each other's gaze. The shopkeeper's bewilderment is so great that his pudgy face seems to go in all directions, like over-risen dough.

'How could you dare?' repeats the priest.

'Who... you mean me, Father?' asks Andrey Andreyich in confusion.

'Do you not understand?!' whispers Father Grigory, stepping back in amazement and throwing up his hands. 'What have you got sitting on your shoulders: a head or some other object? You hand in a note for the altar, but you've written in it a word which would be indecent to utter even on the street! Why are you standing there all goggle-eyed? Surely you know the meaning of that word?'

'You mean whore, Father?' mumbles the shopkeeper, going all red and blinking. 'But the Lord, in his mercy... you know, forgave the whore... prepared her a place... and in the Life of Saint Maria of Egypt it is clear what the meaning of this very word is, excuse me...'

The shopkeeper wants to find another way to justify himself, but gets muddled and starts wiping his lips with his sleeve.

'So this is how you understand things!' Father Grigory exclaims, throwing up his hands. 'But the point is that the Lord forgave – do you understand? – *forgave*, whereas you are judging and speaking ill of her, using an indecent word and heaven knows what else! Your own deceased daughter! You won't find a sin like that in ordinary books, let alone in the Holy Scriptures! Let me tell you again, Andrey: there is no need for philosophising! Philosophising is uncalled for here! If God has given you an enquiring mind, and you cannot control it, then it's better not to try and ponder about things… Don't start pondering, just keep your mouth shut!'

'But she was, you know… excuse me, but she was one of them actresses!' retorts the stunned Andrey Andreyich.

'One of them actresses! Well, whatever she was, you have to forget everything now she is dead, and certainly not mention it in prayer requests!'

'I suppose you are right…' the shopkeeper concedes.

'You should do a penance.' From the back of the altar booms the bass voice of the deacon, who is looking scornfully at Andrey Andreyich's embarrassed face. 'Then you would stop being such a clever clogs! Your daughter was a famous artist. They even wrote about her in the newspapers when she died… Some philosopher you are!'

'Of course… it's not really… a suitable word,' mumbles the shopkeeper, 'but it wasn't judgement I had in mind, Father Grigory, I just wanted to make it more holy… so it would be clearer who you were praying for. People write all kinds of titles in the lists for remembrance, like the infant John, the drowned Pelageya, Egor the warrior, the murdered Pavel and such like… That's what I wanted to do.'

'Unwise, Andrey! God will forgive you, but you should take care next time. The main thing is, don't philosophise, and follow the thinking of other people. Do ten prostrations and then be off with you.'

'Very good, Father,' says the shopkeeper, relieved that the reprimand is now over, his face once again assuming its pompous and self-righteous expression. 'Ten prostrations? Fine, I understand. But now, Father, can I make a request… Seeing that I am still her father… and that, as you know, she was still my daughter, whatever she might have got up to, I, that is… excuse me, but I've been meaning to ask you to conduct a requiem today. And I would like to ask you too, Deacon!'

'Now that's different!' says Father Grigory, taking off his cassock. 'Very praiseworthy. I can approve of that… Well, move along! We will be out in a minute.'

Andrey Andreyich walks away from the altar with an imposing, requiem-like expression on his beetroot face, and goes to stand in the middle of the church. Matvey the warden sets up in front of him a little table with the memorial dish of boiled wheat, and in a little while the requiem begins.

The church is silent. Only the metallic clinking of the censer and the drawn-out singing can be heard… Next to Andrey Andreyich stand Matvey the warden, Makarievna the midwife, and her little son Mitka with the withered arm. There is no one else. The deacon sings badly in an unpleasant muffled bass, but the music and the words are so sad that the shopkeeper gradually begins to lose his prim demeanour and give in to his grief. He is remembering his Mashutka… He remembers that she was born when he was still working as a servant up at the Verkhnye Zaprudy manor house. He had been so busy being a servant that he had not noticed his little girl growing up. That long period during which she had turned into a graceful creature with fair hair and dreamy eyes as big as kopecks had completely passed him by. Like most children of favourite servants, she had been given a genteel education along with the young ladies. For want of anything better to do, the gentry folks had taught her to read and write, and to dance, and he had not interfered in her upbringing at all. Just occasionally, when he happened to bump into her by the front gates or on the landing at the top of the stairs, he would remember that she was his daughter, and so he began to teach her prayers and stories from the Bible, whenever he had some spare time. He was revered for his knowledge of the church rules and the Holy Scriptures even back then! The girl willingly listened to him, no matter how dour and humourless the expression on her father's face. She would yawn as she repeated the prayers after him, but whenever he began to tell her stories, stumbling as he tried to express himself in a more sophisticated way, she would be all ears. Esau's lentils, Sodom's punishment and the misfortunes of the young boy Joseph all made her turn pale and open wide her blue eyes.

And then, when he had given up being a servant, and had opened a shop in the village with the money he had saved, Mashutka had gone away to Moscow with those gentry folk…

She had come to visit her father three years before she died. He could barely recognise her. She was now a slim young woman, with the manners of a young lady, and she dressed like one too. She spoke cleverly, like they do in books, smoked tobacco, and slept until midday. When Andrey Andreyich asked her what she did, she had looked him straight in the eye and boldly declared: 'I am an actress!' Such frankness seemed to the former servant to be the height of cynicism. Mashutka had started to boast about her successes and her life as an actress, but when she saw her father go crimson and spread his hands, she fell silent. And so they spent the next two weeks in silence, not looking at each other until she was about to leave. Before she departed, she begged her father to go for a walk with her along the river bank. And he had given in to her entreaties, despite being aghast at the idea of walking with his actress daughter in broad daylight in front of all those honest people.

'What wonderful scenery you have here!' she had exclaimed, as they were walking along. 'Such beautiful ravines and marshes! Heavens, I had forgotten how lovely my birthplace was!'

And she had burst into tears.

'These places just take up space…' Andrey Andreyich had thought, as he looked blankly at the ravines, not understanding his daughter's feelings of delight. 'You get as much profit from them as milk from a billy goat.'

And she had sobbed and sobbed, inhaling the air deeply, as if she was aware that she did not have much longer to breathe it in…

Andrey Andreyich shakes his head like a horse that has been bitten, and begins to cross himself quickly in order to suppress the painful memories…

'Remember, Lord,' he murmurs, 'your deceased servant, the whore Maria, and forgive her transgressions, deliberate and unintended…'

The indecent word again escapes his lips, but he does not notice: it seems that what has lodged firmly in his consciousness cannot be eased out with a nail, let alone Father Grigory's admonitions! Makarievna sighs and whispers something, drawing in breath, while Mitka with the withered arm becomes lost in thought...

'... where there is no sickness, sorrow or mourning...' resounds the deacon, covering his right cheek with his hand.

A ribbon of blueish smoke rises from the censer and basks in the broad, slanting ray of sunlight cutting across the dark and lifeless emptiness of the church. And it seems that the soul of the deceased girl is being drawn up into that sunbeam together with the smoke. Twisting like a child's curls, the thin streams of smoke rise up towards the window as if dispelling all the pain and sadness that poor soul contained.

BLINY

You will know that bliny[8] have been around for over a thousand years, from the ancient Slavic *ab ovo* as it were... They appeared in the world before the beginning of Russian history, and have lived through it from beginning to end, and beyond any doubt were thought up by Russian brains, just like the samovar was... In anthropology they ought to occupy a position of honour, like the six-and-a-half metre fern or the stone-age knife; and if we do not yet have academic treatises on bliny, it is simply because eating bliny is much easier than racking one's brains about them...

Times change, and ancient customs, costumes and songs have gradually been disappearing from old Rus; much has already disappeared, and is now only of historical interest, while things as inconsequential as bliny occupy in the modern Russian repertoire as solid and comfortable a position as they did a thousand years ago. And there is no prospect of that changing in the future either...

Taking into account the venerable antiquity of bliny and their unusual resilience in the battle with innovation, as has been observed down the centuries, it is annoying to think that these tasty discs made from batter serve only narrow culinary and dietary goals... It is annoying both because of their antiquity and their exemplary, thoroughly spartan resilience... Truly, kitchens and bellies are not worth a thousand years.

As far as I am concerned, I am pretty sure that those garrulous old grandfather bliny have other goals in life apart from gluttony and serving the culinary arts... Apart from the heavy batter which is difficult to digest, there is something higher, perhaps symbolic, or even prophetic hidden in them.... But what precisely?

I do not know, and will never know. This has always been and continues to this day to be a deep and impenetrable *woman's secret*, which is as difficult to unravel as it is to make a bear laugh... Yes, bliny, their meaning and their purpose are a woman's secret, and a secret which no man is going to unravel any time soon. You could write a whole operetta about it!

Russian women have solemnly guarded this secret from prehistoric times, passing it down from generation to generation, but only via their daughters and granddaughters. If, heaven help us, a man should ever discover the secret, something so awful will happen, that not even women can imagine it. No wife, no sister, no daughter…. not a single woman will ever give away this secret, however close you might be to her, however low she might fall. It is impossible to buy or exchange this recipe. A woman will never utter it, either in the heat of passion, or in a state of delirium. In a word, it is the only secret over the course of a thousand years which has not managed to filter through as fine a sieve as the fair sex!

How do you cook bliny? This is not known… Only in the far distant future will this discovery be made, but in the meantime we have to eat what we are given without questions or discussion… It's a secret!

You will say that men also cook bliny… True, but bliny cooked by men are not real bliny. Cold comes out of their pores, they feel like rubber galoshes on the teeth, and they do not taste nearly as good as those cooked by women… Chefs must withdraw and admit defeat…

The cooking of bliny is an exclusively female matter… Chefs should have understood long ago that it is not simply a question of pouring batter into hot frying pans, but a sacred rite, a whole complex system with its own beliefs, traditions, language, prejudices, not to mention joy and suffering… Yes, suffering… If Nekrasov said that Russian women are worn out with suffering, then bliny are partly to blame…

I do not know what the process of cooking bliny consists of, but I do know a little about the secret and solemn ways with which women surround this sacred rite… it is all very mystical, fantastic and even spiritualistic… Looking at a woman cooking bliny, one might think that she is summoning up spirits, or extracting the philosopher's stone from the batter…

Firstly, however educated she might be, no woman will begin cooking bliny on the 13th or on the eve of the 13th, or on the Monday or the day before. On these days bliny never come out well. Many shrewd women start cooking bliny long before Shrovetide in order to avoid this, so that the members of their household have the opportunity to eat bliny also on the Monday before Shrove Tuesday and on the 13th of the month.

Secondly, the mistress of the house will always be found on the eve of bliny day whispering something secretly to the cook. They will whisper and look rapturously at each other, as if they are composing a love letter… After they have finished whispering, they will send the kitchen boy Egorka to the shop to buy yeast… The mistress will then spend a long time looking at the yeast that has been bought, sniff it, and however perfect it is, she is bound to say:

'This yeast will not do. Just you go and tell them to give you something better, you wretched boy…'

The lad will run off and bring back new yeast… Then a large china jar will be produced, into which they will pour water, to be mixed with the yeast and a bit of flour… When the yeast has fermented, the mistress and the cook will turn pale, cover the jar with an old tablecloth and put it in a warm place.

'Keep a watch on it, Matryona, don't doze off…' the mistress will whisper. 'And make sure you keep that jar in a warm place!'

There follows a restless, weary night. Both the mistress and the cook will have insomnia, and if they do happen to fall asleep, they will rave and have terrible dreams… How fortunate you are, men, that you do not cook bliny!

The overcast morning will not have time to grow grey outside the window before the mistress will come running barefoot and dishevelled into the kitchen, still in her nightdress.

'So, how is it doing? What's happening?' she will say, showering Matryona with questions. 'Come on, tell me!'

But Matryona is already standing by the jar and sprinkling buckwheat flour into it…

Thirdly, women are strict about making sure no strangers or men in the household come into the kitchen while the bliny are being cooked… Cooks will not even let in firemen during this time… Coming in, looking and asking questions is not allowed… If anyone should peep into the china jar and say: 'What wonderful batter!', then the bliny will not work when you pour it out! It is not known what women say while they are cooking bliny, or what spells they read out.

Exactly half an hour before the batter is poured into the frying pans, the red-faced and already exhausted cook will pour a little hot water or warm milk into the jar. The mistress is standing right there, and wants to say something, but cannot speak she is so gripped by fear.

The members of the household, meanwhile, will be pacing around the room while they wait for the bliny, and thinking, as they catch sight of the mistress as she runs in and out of the kitchen, that someone is giving birth there, or at the very least getting married.

But finally the first frying pan begins to spit, then the second and the third... The first three bliny, which Egorka can eat, are spoiled... but the fourth, fifth, sixth and so on are put on a plate, covered with a napkin and carried into the dining room to those who hunger and thirst...The mistress, red, beaming, and proud, carries them in herself... You could be forgiven for thinking she is holding not bliny in her hands, but her first-born.

How can you explain this majestic sight? By evening the mistress and the cook are so exhausted they can neither stand nor sit. There is an expression of suffering on their faces... Anything more, it seems, and they will be departing this life...

Such is the external side of this sacred rite. If bliny were only intended for base gluttony, then you would agree that the secrecy, the night that has been described, and the suffering would be incomprehensible... But there is clearly something else going on, however, and that 'something' is carefully hidden.

One has to conclude, looking at the ladies, however, that bliny will hold the key to the solution in the future of some great universal problem.

A clear winter midday… The frost is so hard and crisp that Nadenka, who is holding my hand, has a silvery layer coating the little curls on her temples and the barely noticeable down on her upper lip… Nadenka and I are standing on top of a big hill. From our feet down to the ground below stretches a sloping icy run, which the flirtatious sun is looking at as if it was a mirror. Near us are little toboggans upholstered in bright red cloth.

'Let's go down, Nadezhda Petrovna!' I beg her. 'Just once! I promise you, we won't come to any harm, we'll be fine.'

But Nadenka is faint-hearted. As far as she is concerned, the entire slope from her little galoshes edged with lambskin down to the bottom of the toboggan run is an awful and unbelievably deep abyss. She is struck with fear and holding her breath just from gazing down, because if she were to risk flying off into the abyss on such a flimsy vehicle as a fragile toboggan, it seems she might die or go mad. But, ladies and gentlemen, women are capable of making sacrifices. I'm ready to swear to this a thousand times, either in court, or in front of the author of the new book which is called 'About Women'. Fearing for her life, Nadenka eventually gives in to my entreaties. I sit her down on the toboggan, all pale and trembling, put my arm firmly round her waist and then push off with her into the depths.

The toboggan flies like a bullet at breakneck speed… The air we cut through hits our faces, roars and whistles in our ears, frenziedly grabs at our coat-tails, and seems to want to tear our heads from our shoulders. The wind is so strong we can barely breathe… It seems as if the devil has caught us in his clutches and is dragging us down to hell with a roar… Everything around us melts into one long strip that is tearing along at great speed… Any moment now we will be overturned!

'I love you, Nadya!' I say in a low voice when the roar of the wind and the humming of the runners reach their *forte*.

But now the toboggan starts to go much more slowly, it becomes easier to breathe, and we finally come to a halt. Nadenka is neither dead nor alive. She is pale and can scarcely breathe… I help her to stand up…

'Nothing in the world will make me do that again,' she says, looking at me with wide eyes full of terror. 'I promise you, I almost died!'

A little later she recovers and looks inquiringly into my eyes: did I really utter *those* four words or did she just hear them in the noise of the wind whooshing past? And I, as if nothing had happened, am standing beside her smoking, carefully examining a spot on my glove. She takes my arm and we spend a long time walking round the hill... The mystery is clearly bothering her... Were *those* words said or not? Yes or no? It is a question of dignity, honour... and not something to be joked about! Nadenka keeps looking at my face and answering distractedly, pursing her lips with impatience... One moment her face lights up with happiness and the next it clouds over with dejection... I soon begin to notice that there is a fight going on inside her; it is the female spirit hesitating... She stops and obviously wants to say something, and ask something, but she just cannot summon up the courage...

'You know what?' she says without looking at me. 'I think... I mean...'

'What?' I ask.

'Let's do it again... go down in the toboggan....'

We walk up the steps to the top of the hill... Once more I sit the pale and trembling Nadenka on the toboggan, and once again we hurtle off at breakneck speed; and once again at the fastest and noisiest point of our ride, I say in a low voice: 'I love you, Nadenka!'

When the toboggan stops, Nadenka looks back at the path which we have just taken, then looks intently at my impartial face, and listens to my indifferent voice, and the whole of her little figure is an expression of utter bewilderment...

'What is going on?' is written on her face. 'Those words again! And again it is impossible to understand: did he say them, or did I just hear them?' The lack of an answer is bringing her almost to stupefaction, and taxing her patience... The poor girl does not answer my questions, and is frowning and tapping her little foot nervously.

'Should we go home now?' I ask with a forced yawn...

But – oh, you women! Nadenka again wants to hear those words which are sweet to a woman's ear...

42

'Actually… I like this tobogganning,' she says, going red. 'Shall we go down again?'

She 'likes' doing these runs, and yet as she sits down on the toboggan she is pale, barely able to breathe she is so scared, and shaking like a leaf… To hear those words again, though, she is prepared to go flying into a hundred abysses.

We go down a third time, and I can see her watching my lips to see if they will move. But I put my handkerchief to my lips, cough and blow my nose, although I still manage to utter:

'I love you, Nadya!'

So the mystery remains a mystery!… Nadenka is almost in tears…

When I am accompanying her home after the tobogganing, she dawdles the whole way, looking inquisitively at my impartial expression, and waiting impatiently to see whether I will say those words to her.

'It can't be the wind that said them!' says the expression on her face. 'It's you, my friend, who said them! You!'

But as we come to her house, I begin to say goodbye in the most impartial way possible… She holds out her hand to me slowly, unwillingly, as if she is still expecting something; then after thinking for a minute she pulls it back and says in a firm voice:

'Come for dinner with us!'

I love going out for dinner, so I accept her invitation with alacrity… The dinner is simple but elegant. A glass of vodka, a bowl of steaming soup with macaroni, rissoles and mashed potato and for dessert, puff-pastry pies, which sigh under one's spoon… Add to that a long, searching look from a pair of large black eyes, which keep watch on my face throughout the meal, and you will agree it is a magnificent menu… After dinner, when we are alone for a tête-à-tête, Nadenka ??… She has even gone pale with impatience, while I… I am Bismarck! I continue to pretend that I do not know what is going on… I leave her without hinting at love, and not even pronouncing a single word beginning with the letter 'l'.

The next morning I get a little note: 'If you are going tobogganing today, come by and pick me up. N.' And from then on I punctiliously start going tobogganing every day with Nadenka, and as we fly down in the toboggan, I punctiliously say in a low voice the same words: 'I love you, Nadya!'

Soon Nadenka becomes as addicted to this phrase as if it was opium or morphine. She cannot live without it. She is just as terrified going down the run as before, of course, but what place does danger have now? Take away the toboggan from Nadenka, and she will go down on her knees... As long as she hears those words, she does not care about anything else...

But the words of love still remain a mystery... There are two suspects – the wind and I... Which one of us is guilty Nadenka does not know. Having set off to go tobogganing solo one midday, and lost myself amongst the crowd I see Nadenka approaching the hill and looking out for me... Then she goes timidly up the steps... It is scary for her being on her own, but she has to put it to the test finally: will she hear those wonderfully sweet words when I am not there? I see her getting on to the toboggan, all pale, her mouth open with terror, then shutting her eyes, parting with the world forever and pushing off... 'Zzzz!' go the runners. Whether Nadenka hears those words I do not know... All I see is her getting up from the toboggan looking exhausted and flushed... And one can tell from her face that she herself cannot tell whether she heard anything or not... Her heart has sunk into her boots from the terror of it all, and with it her hearing, her vision and her brain...

Then comes the spring month of March... The sun becomes more affectionate, but the earth greyer and gloomier... Our toboggan run grows dark, loses its sparkle and begins to disintegrate... We have given up doing runs down it. There is nowhere for poor Nadenka to hear those words now. Whoever has given up smoking or kicked a morphine habit will know what that yearning feels like.

One day at dusk I am sitting in my garden, which is next to the house that Nadenka lives in. It is still quite cold, there is snow on the ground, and the trees are leafless, but there is already a whiff of spring in the air... I see Nadenka coming out on to the porch and looking sadly and longingly at the bare trees... The spring wind is blowing straight into her pale, sorrowful face... It reminds her of the wind, whose roar on the toboggan run brought her those four words, and her face becomes sad and tearful, as if asking the wind to bring her those sweet words... I steal

44

up to the bushes, hide behind them, and when a gust of wind blows over to Nadenka over my head, I say in a low voice:

'I love you, Nadya!'

Good gracious, look at what is happening to Nadenka! She gives a cry, a smile lights up her face, and she holds out her arms to the wind… That is all I need… I come out from behind the bushes, and without giving Nadenka the chance to lower her hands and open her mouth wide with astonishment, I run over to her and…

But now allow me to get married.

The snow has not yet left the earth, but spring is already asking to enter your heart. If you have ever recovered from a serious illness, you will be familiar with the blessed state when you are in a delicious state of anticipation, and are liable to smile without any obvious reason. Evidently that is what nature is experiencing just now. The ground is cold, mud and snow squelches under foot, but how cheerful, gentle and inviting everything is! The air is so clear and transparent that if you were to climb to the top of the pigeon loft or the bell tower, you feel you might actually see the whole universe from end to end. The sun is shining brightly, and its playful, beaming rays are bathing in the puddles along with the sparrows. The river is swelling and darkening; it has already woken up and very soon will begin to roar. The trees are bare, but they are already living and breathing.

At a time like this, it is good to get the muddy water in the ditches flowing with a broom or a spade, launch little boats on the water, or chip away at stubborn ice with your heels. It is also good to send pigeons flying up to the top of the sky, or clamber up trees and fix starling boxes in them. Yes, everything is good at this happy time of year, particularly if you are young and love nature, if you are not capricious and hysterical, and if you are not obliged by your work to sit surrounded by four walls from morning to night. It is not good if you are ill, if you are wasting away in some chancellery, or if you are communing with the Muses.

Yes, one should definitely not commune with the Muses in spring.

But have a look at the high spirits and vitality of ordinary people. Panteley Petrovich the gardener decked himself out in a wide-brimmed straw hat at first light, and just cannot part with the little cigar butt he picked up on the path earlier that morning. Look: he is standing in front of the kitchen window with his hands on his hips, telling the cook about the boots he bought the day before. The whole of his long and narrow frame is an expression of smugness and self-importance, which is why all the servants can't abide him. He looks at nature with a consciousness of his superiority over it, and there is something proprietorial, imperious and even contemptuous in his attitude, as if while sitting in his greenhouse or digging in the garden he had discovered something about the plant kingdom which no one else knows.

It would be pointless explaining to him that nature is majestic, terrifying, and full of marvellous wonders, before which proud humans must bow their heads. He thinks he knows everything – all nature's secrets, its charms and its wonders – and so beautiful spring for him is just a slave, like that narrow-chested, emaciated woman who sits in the annexe near the greenhouse and feeds his children lent cabbage soup.

And what about the hunter Ivan Zakharov? He is sitting near the stables on an upturned barrel, in a scruffy wool jacket, with galoshes on his bare feet, making wads for his rifle from old corks. He is getting ready to go hunting. He is imagining in his mind the route he will take, with all the paths, the patches of water under melting ice, and the streams; when he shuts his eyes he can see a long straight row of tall, slender trees, under which he will stand with his rifle, shivering in the evening cold with excitement, and straining his keen ears; he imagines the calls which the roding woodcock will make; he can already hear all the bells pealing in the neighbouring monastery after vespers while he is standing there waiting for the birds to rise… He feels well, and unbelievably, unfathomably happy.

But now take a look at Makar Denisych, the young man who works for General Stremoukhov as a sort of scribe and junior manager. His wages are twice those of the gardener, he wears white shirt-fronts, smokes two-rouble tobacco, is always well-dressed and fed, and whenever he meets the general he has the pleasure of shaking his puffy white hand with the large diamond ring, but nevertheless, he is still unhappy! He is constantly surrounded by books, spends twenty-five roubles subscribing to journals, and is always scribbling away… He writes after dinner every evening when everyone has dozed off, and he hides everything he writes in his big trunk. At the very bottom of this trunk lie neatly folded trousers and waistcoats; on them lie a still unopened packet of tobacco, a dozen little boxes of pills, a crimson scarf, a bar of glycerine soap in yellow wrapping, and all sorts of other things, while at the edges of the trunk reams of scrawled-on paper, and also a few issues of the journal *Our Province*, featuring Makar Denisych's stories and articles, cluster shyly together. The whole district regards him as a poet and writer, they all see something strange about him, and they do not much like him, saying that there is something odd about the way he talks, the way he smokes and the way he walks, and even he once blurted out inopportunely that he was a writer when he was summoned as a witness at the magistrates' court, and he blushed, as if he had stolen a chicken.

Here he comes now, walking slowly down the path in a blue coat, a velveteen cap and a cane in his hand… He will walk about five steps, stop and fix his gaze on the sky, or on the old rook sitting in the fir tree.

The gardener stands with his hands on his hips, the huntsman's face is a picture of concentration, but Makar Denisych is stooping, coughing nervously, and looking as sour as if spring is bearing down and asphyxiating him with its fragrances and its beauty!… His soul is full of trepidation. Instead of joy, delight and hope, spring provokes in him only some vague sorts of desires, which just make him feel uneasy, and so he is walking along, unable to work out what it is he wants. And what exactly is it that he wants?

'Ah, Makar Denisych, hello!' He suddenly hears the voice of General Stremoukhov. 'So, have they not brought the post yet?'

'Not yet, your excellency,' answers Makar Denisych, eyeing the carriage in which the healthy-looking, jovial general is sitting with his small daughter.

'Lovely weather! Proper spring day!' says the general. 'You're going for a walk? Getting inspiration, eh?'

But in his eyes is written: 'Nonentity! Mediocrity!'

'By the way, old chap!' says the general, taking hold of the reins. 'I read a wonderful little story while I was having my coffee this morning! It was a trifling thing, just two pages, but an absolute delight! Shame you don't speak French, or I would have given it to you to read…'

The general is soon recounting the content of the story he has read in laborious detail, and Makar Denisych is listening and feeling awkward, as if it is his fault that he is not a French writer who writes little stories.

'I don't understand why he thought it was so good,' he thinks, as he looks at the receding carriage. 'Trivial, hackneyed content… My stories have much more to them.'

And Makar begins to suffer torment. Authorial pride is a pain which rends the heart; whoever suffers from it can no longer hear the birds sing, see the brilliance of the sun, or see spring… One need only lightly touch this sore point for the whole body to writhe in pain. The tortured Makar walks on, and goes through the garden gate on to the muddy road. Here he comes across Mr Bubentsov, who is hurrying somewhere, his whole body springing up and down in his tall carriage.

'Ah, it's our esteemed writer friend!' he shouts. 'Hello there!'

If Makar Denisych was just a clerk or a junior manager, then no one would have dared talk to him in such a condescending, casual tone, but he is a 'writer', a talentless mediocrity!

People like Mr Bubentsov do not understand anything about art and are not very interested in it, but whenever they happen to come across talentless mediocrities they are pitiless and implacable. They are ready to forgive anyone, but not Makar, that eccentric loser with the manuscripts lying in his trunk. The gardener damaged the old rubber plant, and ruined lots of expensive plants, and the general does nothing and goes on spending money like water; Mr Bubentsov only got down to work once a month when he was a magistrate, then stammered, muddled up the laws, and spoke a lot of rubbish, but all this is forgiven and not noticed; but there is no way that anyone can pass by the talentless Makar, who writes passable poetry and stories, without saying something offensive. No one cares that the general's sister-in-law slaps the maids' cheeks, and swears like a trooper when she is playing cards, that the priest's wife never pays up when she loses, that the landowner Flyugin stole a dog from the landowner Sivobrazov, but the fact that *Our Province* returned a bad story to Makar recently is known to the whole district and has provoked mockery, long conversations and indignation, while Makar Denisych is already being referred to as old Makarka.

If someone does not write the way required, they never try to explain what is wrong, but just say:

'That bastard has gone and written another load of rubbish!'

The thought that people do not understand Makar, that they do not want to and are incapable of understanding him stops him from enjoying spring. For some reason he thinks that if people understood

49

him then everything would be fine. But how can they understand whether he is talented or not if no one in the district ever reads anything, or reads in such a way that it would be better if they read nothing at all? How to explain to General Stremoukhov that the little French story was dull, banal, hackneyed and worthless? How to explain to him, indeed, when he has never read anything except dull little stories?

And how women irritate Makar Denisych!

'Oh, Makar Denisych!' they usually say to him. 'What a shame that you were not at the bazaar today! If you could have seen these two peasants fighting! It was so funny, you probably would have written about it!'

All this is of course very petty, the sort of thing a philosopher would scorn, and not pay any attention to, but Makar is on edge. His heart is full of feelings of loneliness, orphanhood, and grief – the sort of grief experienced by only very lonely people and great sinners. He has never swaggered about with his hands on his hips like the gardener, not once in his life. Just occasionally, about once every five years, when he meets another eccentric loser like him somewhere in the forest, on the road, or on a train, and looks him in the eye, he will suddenly come to life for a moment, as will the other person. They will talk at length, argue, express delight and elation, and laugh, so that any bystander would take them for madmen.

But even these rare occasions do not pass without torment usually. As if in jest, Makar and the loser whom he has met will deny the other has talent, they will not acknowledge each other, they will start envying, hating and irritating each other, and will end up parting as enemies. And thus fades away and is extinguished their youth, without joy, love and friendship, without peace of mind, and without all that the gloomy Makar likes to write about in the evening in moments of inspiration.

And along with youth passes spring.

Soon after returning from Petersburg to his estate of Borisovo, Kunin, a young man of about thirty, and a permanent member in the Peasant Arbitration service, despatched a rider over to Sinkovo to summon the local priest, Father Yakov Smirnov.

About five hours later Father Yakov appeared.

'Very pleased to meet you!' said Kunin, greeting him in the hall. 'It's been a year since I've been living and working here, and I thought it was high time we became acquainted. Do come in! But, er... you're so young!' said Kunin in surprise. 'How old are you?'

'Twenty-eight, sir...' said Father Yakov, limply shaking the out-stretched hand, and blushing for some mysterious reason.

Kunin brought his guest into the study and began to inspect him.

'What a gauche, effeminate face!' he thought.

There really was something 'womanish' in Father Yakov's face: a snub nose, scarlet cheeks and large grey-blue eyes with sparse, barely perceptible eyebrows. His long red hair fell lankly and listlessly to his shoulders in straight locks. His moustache had only just begun to grow into a proper man's moustache, while his beard belonged to the sort of useless beards which seminary students for some reason call a 'scratching': it was thin and extremely weedy; you could not stroke it or use a comb on it, you could only pluck at it... All this meagre growth sat unevenly, in clumps, as if Father Yakov had thought of making himself up to look like a priest but had been interrupted half-way through sticking on the beard. He was wearing a cassock the colour of weak chicory coffee, with large patches on each elbow.

'Strange individual...' thought Kunin, looking at his mud-spattered hems. 'He comes into the house for the first time and can't even manage to dress decently.'

'Sit down, Father!' he said, in a familiar rather than friendly tone, pulling up a chair to his desk. 'Do sit down, please!'

Father Yakov coughed into his fist, lowered himself awkwardly on to the edge of the chair and placed his palms on his knees. Sunken-chested and rather puny, his face red and perspiring, he made a sin-gularly unpleasant impression on Kunin to begin with. Kunin would have never believed before that there were such feeble and pathetic-looking priests in Russia, and he saw a lack of dignity and even obsequiousness in Father Yakov's posture, in his manner of keeping his palms on his knees, and sitting on the edge of his seat.

'I've invited you here, Father, on business...' began Kunin, leaning back into his armchair. 'The pleasant duty of helping you in one of your worthy ventures has fallen to me... The fact is that when I returned from Petersburg, I found on my desk a letter from our local marshal. Egor Dmitrievich has proposed that I take under my guardianship the parish school you are setting up in Sinkovo. I'm very glad, Father, really, with all my heart... More than that, I am delighted to accept this proposal!'[9]

Kunin stood up and walked around the study.

'Of course, both Egor Dmitrievich and probably you as well will know that I don't have extensive funds at my disposal. My estate is mortgaged, and I live only on my Permanent Member's salary. So you cannot count on me for any major help, but I will do whatever is in my powers... So when do you plan to open the school, Father?'

'When we have the money...' answered Father Yakov.

'And what means do you have at your disposal currently?'

'Almost none at all, sir... The peasants decided at the assembly that each male would contribute thirty kopecks each year, but that is only a pledge after all! And to obtain basic equipment we need at least two hundred roubles...'

'Mmm, I see... Unfortunately I don't have that sort of sum at the moment...' sighed Kunin. 'I spent everything on the journey here and... even had to borrow some. Let's both put our heads together and think of something.'

Kunin started to think out loud. He put forward his opinions, and scrutinised Father Yakov's face, looking for approval or agreement. But his face was blank and impassive, and expressed nothing but shy diffidence and uneasiness. Looking at him, you might have thought that Kunin was talking about abstruse things which Father Yakov did not understand, and which he was listening to only out of politeness, fearing his ignorance would be exposed.

'This chap is clearly not one of the brightest...' thought Kunin. 'He's excessively shy and slow-witted.'

Only when a servant came into the study, and brought in on a tray two glasses of tea and a sugar-bowl full of biscuits did Father Yakov liven up a little and even smile. He took his glass and started immediately to drink from it.

'Shouldn't we write to His Grace?' Kunin said, continuing to think aloud. 'After all, strictly speaking, it's not the zemstvo, and not us, but the higher church authorities who raised the question of parish schools. They should be allocating the funds, really. I seem to remember reading somewhere that some kind of sum was being assigned for this purpose. Do you know anything about it?'

Father Yakov was so engrossed in drinking his tea that he did not immediately answer the question. He raised his grey-blue eyes to Kunin, thought for a while, and then, as if he had just remembered the question, shook his head. An expression of pleasure and appetite, of the most commonplace, everyday kind, stretched across his unattractive face from ear to ear. He relished every gulp he drank. After drinking every last drop, he put the glass on the desk, then took it back again, looked at the bottom of the glass, and then put it back again... Then Kunin saw his guest take a biscuit from the sugar bowl, take a bite out of it, turn it over in his hands and then quickly slip it into his pocket.

'Now that really is clerical behaviour!' thought Kunin, shrugging his shoulders with distaste. 'What is this, priestly greed or childishness?'

Having let his guest drink another glass of tea and showed him to the door, Kunin lay down on the sofa and surrendered to the unpleasant feeling produced by Father Yakov's visit.

'What a strange, outlandish person!' he thought. 'Dirty, scruffy, rude, stupid, and probably drinks too... Goodness, and this is a priest, a man of the cloth! A minister to the people! I can only imagine the irony in the deacon's voice as he proclaims to him before every service: "Give us the blessing, Father!" A good clergyman he is! A clergyman who has not a shred of dignity, uneducated, hiding biscuits in his pockets like a schoolboy... Good gracious, where were the bishop's eyes looking when he ordained this fellow? Who do they take the people for if they give them such instructors? They need people who...'

And Kunin started thinking about what Russian priests should be like....

'Now if I were a priest, for example... A priest who is educated and loves his work can achieve a lot... I would have had the school opened long ago. And preaching? Well if a priest is sincere and inspired by love for his work, then he can compose wonderful, rousing sermons!'

Kunin closed his eyes and started mentally putting together a sermon. A little while later he was sitting at his desk and quickly setting it down on paper.

'I'll give this to old ginger hair, and he can read it out in church...' he thought.

The following Sunday morning, Kunin drove over to Sinkovo to sort out the school problem once and for all, and also to get to know the church of which he was a parishioner. Despite the spring mud on the roads, the morning was glorious. The sun was shining brightly and piercing the white patches of snow which still lay about with its rays. In its farewell to the earth, the snow was sparkling with so many diamonds that it was painful to look at, while near it the winter crops were hurrying to turn green. Rooks were flying solemnly over the earth. One rook flew by, descended to the ground, and jumped up and down a few times before standing on its legs...

The wooden church which Kunin drove up to was grey and dilapidated: the columns by the porch which had once been whitewashed were now all peeling and looked like two ugly shafts. The icon above the door just looked like a dark patch. But Kunin found this poverty touching and affecting. Lowering his eyes modestly, he went into the church and stopped by the door. The service had only just begun. An old sexton, bent over double, was intoning the hours in a muffled, indistinct tenor. Father Yakov, conducting the service without the deacon, was walking around the church with the censer. If Kunin had not been overcome with humility as he walked into the poverty-stricken church, he would definitely have smiled at the sight of Father Yakov. The puny clergyman was wearing a grubby and incredibly long vestment made out of some kind of threadbare yellow material. The hem trailed along the ground.

The church was not full. To begin with, Kunin was struck by a strange circumstance as he looked at the congregation: he could only see old people and children... But after standing there for a while, and looking more intently at the old faces, Kunin saw that he had taken young people for old. He did not pay this small optical illusion any particular attention, however.

The interior of the church was as old and grey as the exterior. There was not one spot on the iconostasis and on the brown walls which was not blackened with soot or showing wear and tear. There were many windows, but the general colour seemed grey, so there was a permanent twilight in the church.

'He who is pure in heart will pray well here...' thought Kunin. 'St Peter's in Rome may strike us with majesty, and here we are moved by humility and simplicity.'

But his prayerful mood dissolved into the smoke when Father Yakov entered the sanctuary and began the Liturgy. Because he was so young and had become a priest straight from the seminary bench, Father Yakov had not yet mastered a distinct manner of conducting a service. As he read, he seemed to be deciding which kind of voice to use, a high tenor or a thin little bass; he bowed ineptly, walked quickly, opened and closed the Royal Doors by fits and starts... And the old sacristan, who was clearly deaf as well as sick, did not hear his proclamations well, which led to minor confusions. Father Yakov would barely manage to read his bit, and already the sacristan was singing his response, or else Father Yakov would come to a halt, and the old man would be straining his ear in the direction of the altar, listening out and staying silent, until people tugged on his cassock. The old man had an unhealthy, muffled, tremulous voice with a lisp, and he was short of breath... To complete the sorry scene, the sacristan was ushered about by a very small boy whose head could barely be seen from behind the rail of the choir-stall. The boy sang in a shrill high descant and seemed to be trying not to sing in tune. Kunin stood for a while listening, then went outside for a smoke. He was already disillusioned, and now looked at the grey church almost with hostility.

'And they complain about the lapse in religious feeling amongst the people...' he sighed. 'I should say so! They should install more priests like that here!'

Kunin went into the church about three more times, and every time he had a strong desire to go outside for some fresh air. He waited until the end of the service and then set off to see Father Yakov. On the out-side, the priest's house was no different from the peasant izbas, except that the straw on the roof was a bit more even, and there were little white curtains in the windows. Father Yakov led Kunin into a small bright room with a clay floor, and walls on which some cheap wall-paper had been stuck. Despite a few attempts at luxury, such as photo-graphs in frames and a clock with scissors attached to the pendulum, the furnishing was noticeable for its general impoverishment. Looking at the furniture, one might have thought that Father Yakov had gone the rounds of all the nearby households, collecting it piece by piece: in one place he had been given a round table on three legs, in another a stool, in a third a chair whose back leaned too much, in the fourth a chair with a straight back, while in the fifth they had clearly gone to town and donated a semblance of a couch with a flat back and checked cushions. This semblance was painted dark red and smelled strongly of paint. Kunin wanted to sit on one of the chairs at first, then thought about it and sat on the stool.

'Was this the first time you came to our church?' asked Father Yakov, hanging his hat on an ugly big nail.

'Yes, it was. You know, Father… Before we sit down to business, would you give me a cup of tea, I am completely parched.'

Father Yakov blinked, grunted, and then went behind the partition. Whispering could be heard…

'That must be his wife…' thought Kunin. 'It would be interesting to see what sort of a wife old ginger hair has got.'

A little while later Father Yakov came out from behind the partition all red and perspiring. Trying hard to smile, he sat down on the edge of the couch opposite Kunin.

'The samovar will be lit in a minute,' he said, not looking at his guest.

'Good heavens, they haven't even started heating the samovar!' thought Kunin to himself in horror. 'I'm going to have to wait a long time for my tea!'

'I've brought you a draft of the letter I wrote to the bishop. I'll read it after we have had tea… Maybe you will want to add something…'

'Very well, sir.'

Silence ensued. Father Yakov looked apprehensively out of the corner of his eye at the partition, arranged his hair and blew his nose.

'Wonderful weather…' he said.

'Yes. By the way, I read an interesting thing yesterday… The Volsk[9] zemstvo has proposed handing over all its schools to the clergy. It's typical.'

Kunin stood up, started pacing over the clay floor and began expressing his opinions.

'That in itself is alright,' he said, 'as long as the clergy rises to the challenge of its vocation and clearly recognises its duties. To my great misfortune, I know priests whose level of education and moral qualities would not qualify them as military clerks, let alone priests. And you have to agree that a bad teacher will bring rather less harm to a school than a bad priest.'

Kunin glanced at Father Yakov. The latter was sitting hunched over, thinking hard about something, and evidently not listening to his guest.

'Yasha, will you come here!' a woman's voice sounded from behind the partition. The whispering began again.

Kunin longed desperately for some tea.

'No, I'm never going to get any tea here!' he thought, looking at his watch. 'In fact it seems I am not exactly a welcome guest. My host has not deigned to share a single word with me, and he just sits there blinking.'

Kunin reached for his hat, waited until Father Yakov came back and then took his leave.

'That was a wasted morning!' he thought to himself angrily on his way home. 'Numbskull! Blockhead! He has as much interest in the school as I have in last year's snow. No, I'm not going to be able to work with him! Nothing will happen from anything we do together! If the marshal knew what sort of priest they had here, he would be in no hurry to trouble about the school. You need to worry about a good priest first, and only then think about a school!'

Kunin now almost hated Father Yakov. That man, that pathetic, ludicrous figure in the crumpled long cassock, his effeminate face, his manner of conducting services, his way of life and his bureaucratic, timorous deference offended that small remnant of religious feeling which still remained in his heart, and which quietly glowed together with the stories he had been told by his nanny. The coldness and brusqueness with which he had greeted the sincere, ardent interest that Kunin had taken in his affairs, meanwhile, was hard for his pride to take.

Later that evening Kunin paced from room to room for a long time thinking, but then sat down decisively at his desk and wrote the bishop a letter. As well as asking for money for the school, and his blessing, he offered in passing, like a good son, his sincere opinion of the Sinkovo priest. 'He's young,' he wrote; 'not sufficiently educated, it appears, is given to drink, and generally does not meet the expectations which over the centuries the Russian people have formed with reference to their pastors.' Kunin gave a light sigh after finishing this letter, and went to bed knowing he had done a good thing.

On Monday morning, while he was still lying in bed, he was informed that Father Yakov had arrived. He did not feel like getting up, so he ordered his servant to say he was not at home. On Tuesday he went away to a meeting, and when he returned on Saturday found out from his servants that Father Yakov had come every day.

'I remember how much he liked my biscuits!' thought Kunin.

Father Yakov came on Sunday in the late afternoon. This time, not only his hems but even his hat was spattered with mud. Like on his first visit, his face was red and perspiring, and he sat down, like before, on the very edge of the chair. Kunin resolved not to start talking about the school, so as not to waste time idly.

'Pavel Mikhailovich, I've brought you a list of school textbooks...' began Father Yakov.

'Thank you.'

But it was quite clear that Father Yakov had not come on account of the list. He exuded an intense embarrassment, but at the same time, like a person who has suddenly been struck by a great idea, his face expressed decisiveness. He was striving to say something important and extremely necessary, and was now battling to conquer his timidity.

'Why is he silent?' thought Kunin angrily. 'He's settled in here! But I don't have the time to hang about with him!'

In order to smooth the awkwardness of his silence and conceal the struggle going on inside him, the priest began to force a smile, and this

58

protracted smile, forced out through the perspiration and redness of his face, and which did not fit with the fixed glance of his grey-blue eyes, forced Kunin to avert his gaze. He felt disgusted.

'I'm sorry, Father, but I have to leave…' he said.

Father Yakov gave a start, like a sleepy person who has been hit, and began in embarrassment to gather up the hems of his cassock, continuing still to smile. Despite all the aversion he felt towards this man, Kunin suddenly started to feel sorry for him, and decided he should be less callous.

'Please come another time though, Father…' he said. 'And I've got a request to make as you leave… I sort of got inspired, you see, and wrote two sermons. I want to give them to you to have a look at… If they are any good, you could read them.'

'Alright…' said Father Yakov, covering with his hand Kunin's sermons, which lay on the desk. 'I'll take them…'

After standing there for a while, still gathering up the folds of his crumpled cassock, he suddenly dropped the forced smile and raised his head decisively.

'Pavel Mikhailovich,' he said, clearly trying to speak loudly and clearly.

'What can I do for you?'

'I've heard that you have sacked, er… dismissed your clerk and…and are looking for a new one…'

'Yes, I am… Do you have someone you can recommend?'

'I, er… you see, well… Would you be able to give the job to me?'

'Are you planning on giving up being a priest?' said Kunin in amazement.

'No, no,' said Father Yakov hastily, for some reason going pale, and trembling all over. 'Heaven preserve me! If you have doubts, then don't worry about it, really. I could fit it in with my work, you see… and add to my income… But it's not important, don't worry!'

'Hmm… income… But I only pay my clerk twenty roubles a month!'

'Goodness, I'd do it for ten!' whispered Father Yakov to himself. 'And ten would be enough! You… you are amazed, like everyone is. Greedy, grasping priest, you think, what does he want with the money?

I feel myself that I am greedy... and I punish myself, I condemn it... it's hard to look people in the eye... I'm telling you the truth, Pavel Mikhailovich... may God be my witness...'

Father Yakov drew breath and went on.

'I prepared for you a whole confession on my way here, but... I've forgotten it, and can't find the words. I receive a hundred and fifty roubles a year from the parish, and everyone... wonders what I do with all that money... But I'll explain it all to you frankly... I contribute forty roubles a year for my brother Pyotr at the seminary. Everything else is provided for him there, but the pens and paper are mine...'

'I believe you, I believe you! But what's the point of all this?' said Kunin with a wave of his hand, feeling the terrible burden of his guest's openness, and not knowing how to deal with the tears glistening in his eyes.

'Then I haven't paid back the consistory fully for sorting out my position. They took two hundred roubles from me for the position, and I have to pay back twenty a month... So you can judge for yourself, what is left? And apart from all that, I then also have to give Father Avraam at least three roubles a month!'

'What Father Avraam are we talking about?'

'Father Avraam who served as the priest in Sinkovo before me. They relieved him of his post because of his... weakness, but he is still living in Sinkovo! Where is he supposed to go? Who is going to feed him? He might be old, but he needs coal, and bread, and clothing! I cannot allow a priest to go begging! It would be a sin on my conscience! A sin! He...has borrowed from everyone, but it would be a sin for me not to pay for him.'

Father Yakov leapt up, and started pacing from one corner to the other, staring wildly at the floor. 'God in heaven!' he murmured, lifting his hands and then dropping them. 'Save us, Lord, and have mercy! Why take holy orders, when I had little faith and was lacking in strength? There is no end to my despair! Save me, O Mother of God.'

'Calm down, Father!' said Kunin.

'I'm racked by hunger, Pavel Mikhailovich!' continued Father Yakov. 'Be generous and forgive me, but I have no more strength... I know that if I bow my head and ask, anyone would help, but... I can't! I'm ashamed! How can I ask from the peasants? You work here, so you can see for yourself... Who could ask from beggars? And I can't ask from people better off, from the landowners! Pride! I'm ashamed!'

Father Yakov gave a wave of his hand and scratched his head nervously with both hands.

'I'm ashamed! Goodness, how ashamed I am! I'm too proud to let people see my poverty! When you came to visit me, Pavel Mikhailovich, there wasn't any tea you know! There wasn't even the slightest hint of it, but pride stopped me confessing it to you! I'm ashamed of my clothes, these patches... I'm ashamed of my vestments, my hunger... But is it decent for a priest to have pride?'

Father Yakov stopped in the middle of the study and started reasoning with himself, as if he was unaware of Kunin's presence.

'Well, suppose I were to deal with the hunger and the shame, I've still got my wife to think about! I took her from a good home, after all! She is well brought up and refined, she is used to tea and white rolls, and to laundered sheets... She used to play the piano when she was living with her parents... She is young, not even twenty yet... She must want to dress up, enjoy herself, socialise... But with me... she is worse than any cook, and it's shameful to show her on the street. Oh God, oh God! Her only pleasure is when I bring her an apple or a nice biscuit after I've been visiting someone...'

Father Yakov again started scratching his head with both hands.

'And it's not love we have between us, but pity... I can't look at her without compassion! To think of what goes on in the world. People wouldn't believe it if they wrote about it in the newspapers... And when will it come to an end?'

'That's enough, Father!' Kunin almost shouted, scared of his tone. 'Why look so gloomily at life?'

'Please forgive me, Pavel Mikhailovich...' mumbled Father Yakov, as if drunk. 'It's nothing, please don't pay any attention... I'm the one to blame, and I will go on blaming myself... I will!'

Father Yakov looked around and whispered:

'I was walking early one morning from Sinkovo to Luchkovo, and I could see a woman doing something on the river bank... I went up closer and could not believe my eyes... What a nightmare! The wife

61

of Ivan Sergeyich, the doctor, was sitting there washing her linen… The doctor's wife, who graduated from the institute! It meant that she had contrived to get up early and walk half a mile out of the village, so people would not see her… Indomitable pride! When she saw that I was there and had noticed her poverty, she went bright red… I was struck dumb, and took fright, but I ran up to her, wanting to help her, and she hid her linen from me, scared I would see her tattered nightgowns.'

'All this is somehow hard even to comprehend…' said Kunin, sit-ting down and looking almost in horror at Father Yakov's pale face.

'Yes, it's hard to comprehend! It's never happened before that a doctor's wife had to do her laundry by the river! That doesn't happen in any other country! As a pastor and spiritual father, I shouldn't allow such things to happen, but what can I do? What? I myself try and get free treatment from her husband! You're right to say that this is hard to comprehend! One can't believe one's eyes! During the Liturgy, you know, when I look out from the altar and see my congregation, and hungry Avraam and his wife, and when I remember the doctor's wife, and how her hands went blue from the icy water, then believe me, I lose my train of thought and stand there like an idiot, in complete oblivion until the sacristan responds… It's terrible!'

Father Yakov started pacing around the room again.

'Lord Jesus!' he said, throwing up his hands. 'And all the holy saints! I'm incapable of even conducting services… Here you are telling me about a school, and I'm standing there like a stuffed dummy, not understanding anything and only thinking about food… Even when I'm before the altar too… Anyway… whatever am I doing?' Father Yakov suddenly remembered. 'You have to leave. Forgive me, it's just that I…I'm sorry.'

Kunin shook Father Yakov's hand silently, accompanied him to the hall, came back into his study and stopped in front of the window. He watched Father Yakov leave the house, pull his wide-brimmed rust-coloured hat down on his head, and quietly set off down the road, his head bowed, as if ashamed of having been so open.

'I can't see his horse,' thought Kunin.

Kunin was afraid to confront the fact that the priest had been coming to his house on foot these past days: it was nearly five miles to Sinkov, and the mud on the road was frightful. Then Kunin saw Andrei the coachman and the boy Paramon jumping over puddles and spattering Father Yakov with mud as they ran up to him to receive a blessing. Father Yakov took off his hat and slowly blessed Andrey, then blessed the boy and stroked his head.

Kunin passed his hand over his eyes, and it seemed to him that his hand had become damp. He walked away from the window and with blurry eyes looked around the room, still hearing the timid, stifled voice... He looked at his desk... Fortunately, in his haste Father Yakov had forgotten to take his sermons with him... Kunin pounced on them, tore them into shreds and flung them under the desk with disgust.

'And I didn't know!' he groaned, falling on to the sofa. 'I, who have been serving for over a year here as a Permanent Member, as an honorary magistrate, as a member of the schools committee! Blind idiot, numbskull! You've got to help them right away! Right away!'

He squirmed in agony, then squeezed his temples and focused his thoughts.

'I'll get two hundred roubles salary on the 20th... I'll find some excuse to slip him and the doctor's wife something... I'll ask him to hold a service here, and will pretend to the doctor that I am ill... That way I won't hurt their pride. And I'll help Avraam...'

He counted up his money on his fingers and was afraid to admit to himself that those two hundred were barely enough for him to pay his steward, the servants, and the peasant who brought the meat... He could not help but remember the not too distant past, when he had foolishly squandered his father's money, when as a twenty-year-old raw youth he would give prostitutes expensive fans, pay Kuzma the cabman ten roubles a day, and bring actresses gifts purely for vanity's sake. Ah, to what good use he could put all those frittered roubles now, all those three-rouble, ten-rouble notes!

'Father Avraam only lives on three roubles a month,' thought Kunin. 'The priest's wife can sew herself a nightgown for a rouble, and the doctor can pay a laundress. But nevertheless, I will help! I will definitely help!'

Then Kunin suddenly remembered the denunciation he had written to the bishop, and he grimaced, as if hit by a sudden blast of cold air.

This recollection filled his soul with a feeling of deep shame both before himself and the invisible truth... So began and ended the genuine inclination to useful activity of one well-intentioned but thoroughly complacent and not terribly thoughtful person.

The rooks have returned and are circling in flocks over Russian pastures.[10] I chose the most respectable-looking of them and began a conversation with him. Unfortunately I had stumbled across a rook who was a hardened moralist, and so the conversation was dull. Here is what we talked about:

I: They say that you rooks live for a very long time. How old are you?

Rook: I am three hundred and seventy-six years old.

I: Oh! You don't say! Well, you've certainly been around for a while, that's for sure! If I had been in your shoes, sir, heaven knows how many articles I would have sent off to *Russian Antiquity* and *Historical Bulletin*! If I live until I'm 376, I imagine I would have written by that time tons of stories, sketches and little dramas! To think of the royalties I would have earned! So rook, what have you been doing all this time?

Rook: Nothing, Mr Human Being! I have just drunk, eaten, slept and multiplied...

I: How shameful! I feel ashamed and sorry for you, stupid bird! You have lived on earth for 376 years, and are as stupid as you were three hundred years ago! You haven't progressed one tiny bit!

Rook: Wisdom, Mr Human Being, comes from education and the way one is brought up, not from longevity. Take China, for example... It has lived a lot longer than me, and yet has remained as much a twit as it was a thousand years ago.

I (continuing to be amazed): 376 years! That's a long time you know! A whole eternity! In that time I would have managed to spend time in every university faculty, I'd have got married twenty times, I would have had time to try out every possible career and job, I would have gone up through the ranks in the civil service to I don't know where, and probably would have died a proper Rothschild! After all, get this, you fool: one rouble invested in the bank at 5% compound interest in 283 years will turn into a million! Work it out! So if you had paid in to your account one rouble 283 years ago, you would have a million now! What a fool you are! And aren't you ashamed and angry at how stupid you are?

Rook: Not at all... We may be stupid, but we can console ourselves that over the 400 years of our lifetime we have done fewer stupid things than man has in forty... Oh yes, Mr Human Being! I've been living for 376 years, but have never once seen rooks fighting each other and killing each other, while you can't even remember a year in which there was

no war going on... We do not rob each other, we do not offer loans at interest, and schools which do not teach classics, we do not slander, or blackmail, we do not write bad novels and poems, or publish scurrilous newspapers... I have lived for 376 years and have never seen lady rooks deceive and offend their husbands, but what about with you, Mr Human Being? We don't have servants, toadies, lackies, traitors amongst us, moreover...

But just then my companion's comrades called to him, and he flew off over the pasture without finishing his tirade.

GRISHA

Grisha, a chubby little boy born two years and eight months ago, is going for a walk along the boulevard with his nanny. He is wearing a long quilted cape, a big hat with a furry button, and warm galoshes. He is feeling hot and sticky, and the bright April sun is beating down too, shining right in his eyes and stinging his eyelids.

As he walks timidly and hesitantly along, his clumsy figure is an expression of utter bewilderment.

Until now Grisha has only known a four-sided world where his bed stands in one corner, Nanny's trunk is in another, there is a chair in the third, and an icon lamp is burning in the fourth. If you look under the bed, you will see a doll with a broken-off hand, and a drum, and behind Nanny's trunk there are lots of different things: cotton reels, bits of paper, a basket without a lid, and a broken clown. Apart from Nanny and Grisha, Mama and the cat are often in this world. Mama looks like a doll, and the cat looks like Papa's fur coat, except that it does not have any eyes or a tail. From the world which is called the nursery, the door leads into a space where they have lunch and drink tea. This is where Grisha's chair stands on tall legs, and where on the wall there is a clock, which exists only to swing its pendulum and chime. From the dining room you can go into a room where there are mahogany armchairs. There is a dark patch on the carpet here which they still wag their fingers at Grisha about. Beyond this room there is another one, which they do not let him go into, but which Papa makes brief visits to sometimes – he is a highly mysterious person! Nanny and Mama are understandable – they dress Grisha, feed him, and put him to bed, but why Papa exists is not known. There is another mysterious person – Auntie, who gave Grisha a drum. She appears and disappears. Where does she disappear to? Grisha has looked a few times under the bed, behind the trunk and under the couch, but she was not there…

In this new world, where the sun hurts your eyes, there are so many Papas, Mamas and Aunties that you do not know whom to run to. But the horses are the strangest and most absurd thing. Grisha looks at their moving legs and does not understand anything. He looks at Nanny, hoping she will dispel his confusion, but she is silent.

Suddenly he hears a frightening tramping sound… Along the boulevard, walking evenly, a crowd of soldiers with red faces and with bundles of birch twigs under their arms is bearing straight down on him. Grisha freezes with horror and looks inquiringly at Nanny: are they in danger? But Nanny does not run or cry, so it must mean they are not in danger. Grisha follows the soldiers with his eyes and begins to fall into line with them.

Two large cats with long faces, sticking-out tongues and tails in the air run across the boulevard. Grisha thinks that he has to run too, so he starts running after the cats.

'Stop!' Nanny shouts at him, grabbing him roughly by the shoulder. 'Where are you off to? Since when were you allowed to be so naughty?'

Here is a kind of nanny sitting with a small tub of oranges. Grisha walks past her and quietly takes an orange for himself.

'What do you think you are doing?' his companion shouts, slapping him on the hand and wrenching the orange from him. 'You fool!'

Now Grisha would love to pick up the piece of glass lying under his feet, which sparkles like the icon lamp, but he is afraid his hand will be slapped again.

'My compliments to you!' All of a sudden Grisha hears someone's loud, deep voice right above his ear, and he sees a tall person with shiny buttons.

To his great pleasure, this person shakes hands with Nanny, stops and begins to talk to her. The sunshine, the noise of the carriages, the horses, and the shiny buttons are all so amazingly new and unscary that Grisha's heart fills with pleasure, and he begins to laugh.

'Let's go! Let's go!' he shouts to the man with shiny buttons, pulling on his coat tails.

'Where are we going?' asks the person.

'Let's go!' Grisha insists.

He wants to say that it would not be at all bad to take along Papa, Mama and the cat too, but his tongue does not say what is needed.

A little later, Nanny turns off the boulevard and takes Grisha into a big courtyard where there is still snow. And the man with shiny buttons also goes with them. They carefully bypass lumps of snow and puddles, then they go up a dirty, dark staircase, and into a room. There is a lot of smoke here, it smells of stew, and a woman is standing by the stove frying rissoles. The cook and Nanny kiss each other, then they sit down with the man on a bench and begin talking quietly. Grisha begins to feel unbearably hot and stuffy wrapped up still in his coat.

'Why are we here?' he thinks, looking round.

He sees a dark ceiling, an oven fork with two prongs, and a stove which looks out with its large black cavity...

'Ma-a-ma!' he cries with longing.

'Now, now!' shouts Nanny. 'You can wait a bit!'

The cook puts a bottle, three glasses and a pie on the table. The two women and the man with shiny buttons clink glasses and drink several times, and the man keeps embracing the nanny and the cook. And then all three begin to sing softly.

Grisha reaches out for the pie, and they give him a piece. He eats and watches Nanny drinking... He would like a drink too.

'I want some, Nanny! I want some!' he asks.

The cook lets him take a sip from her glass. He screws up his eyes, pulls a face, coughs and then waves his arms around for a long time, while the cook looks at him and laughs.

When they return home, Grisha starts to tell Mama, the walls and the bed about where he has been, and what he has seen. He speaks not so much with his tongue as with his face and hands. He shows how the sun shines, how the horses trot, how the scary stove watches you, and how the cook drinks...

In the evening he cannot fall asleep. The soldiers with birch twigs, the big cats, the horses, the piece of glass, the tub of oranges, the shiny buttons – all this has gathered into a bundle and is pressing on his brain. He tosses from side to side, talks to himself, and, unable to bear his state of excitement, eventually starts crying.

'You've got a fever!' says his Mama, touching his forehead with her palm. 'How can that have happened?'

'The stove!' cries Grisha. 'Go away stove!'

'It must be something you ate...' decides Mama.

And Grisha, bursting with the impressions of the new life he has only just experienced for the first time, receives from his Mama a spoonful of castor oil.

I was standing on the banks of the Goltva and waiting for the ferry to arrive from the other side. Most of the time the Goltva is a pretty average sort of river – silent, pensive, glistening meekly behind thick reeds – but now a whole lake stretched before me. The swollen spring waters had broken both banks, and had flooded a long way beyond them on both sides, taking in vegetable gardens, hayfields and marshes, so that there were quite a few lone poplars sticking up through the surface of the water, and bushes which looked like austere cliffs in the darkness.

I thought the weather was absolutely marvellous. It was dark, but I could still see trees, water and people... The world was lit up with stars which were scattered throughout the entire sky. I do not remember ever seeing so many stars before. There was literally no space even to poke a finger. There were stars as big as goose eggs, and ones as small as hempseed... From the smallest to the biggest, they had come out into the sky one by one to celebrate Easter, all clean, rejuvenated and joy-ful, and every single one of them was quietly twinkling. The sky was reflected in the water; the stars bathed in the dark depths and shimmered along with its light ripple. The air was warm and quiet... Far away, on the other bank, in pitch darkness, a few bright red lights were dotted about here and there...

A few feet away from me was the dark silhouette of a peasant in a tall hat and a thick gnarled stick.

'The ferry is a long time coming!' I said.

'It should be here about now,' replied the silhouette.

'Are you also waiting for the ferry?'

'No, I'm just standing here...' yawned the peasant. 'Waiting for the luminations. I'd go over, but I don't have five kopecks for the ferry.'

'I'll give you five kopecks.'

'No, it's alright, thanking you humbly... You'd best light a candle for me in the monastery with those five kopecks... That would be more interesting, and I'll just stop here. Lord have mercy on us, what's happened to that ferry? It's like it's vanished into thin air!'

The peasant went up to the water's edge, took the cable in his hand and shouted:

'Ieronim! Ieroni-im!'

As if in reply to his yell, the long drawn-out sound of the great bell came over from the other bank. The sound was rich and deep, like from the thickest string on a double bass: it seemed that the darkness itself was wheezing. Just then a shot was also fired from a cannon. It resounded in the darkness and ended up somewhere a long way behind my back. The peasant took off his hat and crossed himself.

'Christ is risen!' he said.

The waves of sound from the first peal of the bell had barely managed to stop in the air when another could be heard, and after that there was immediately a third, and the darkness was filled with a constant, vibrating hum. New lights started burning near the red lights, and they all started to shimmer, flickering restlessly.

'Ieroni-im!' came a long drawn-out, muffled cry.

'They are shouting from the other bank,' said the peasant. 'So the ferry isn't there either. Our Ieronim has fallen asleep.'

The lights and the velvet sound of the bell were mesmerising... I had begun to lose patience and get agitated, but then as I peered into the dark distance I finally saw the silhouette of something which looked very like a gallows. It was the long awaited ferry. It was moving so slowly, that if it had not been gradually coming into view, one might have thought it was standing in one place or going to the other bank.

'Hurry up, Ieronim!' shouted my peasant. 'The gentleman's waiting!'

The ferry crept towards the bank, rolled, and then stopped with a screech. A tall man in a monk's habit and a conical hat was standing on it, holding on to the cable.

'What took you so long?' I asked, jumping on to the ferry.

'In Christ's name, forgive me,' Ieronim replied quietly. 'There's no one else?'

'No...'

Ieronim took the cable with both hands, bent himself into a question mark and grunted. The ferry creaked and began to roll. The silhouette of the peasant in the tall hat began slowly to recede from me, which meant the ferry had started to move. Ieronim soon straightened up and began to work the cable with one hand. We were silent and just gazed at the bank towards which we were travelling. The 'luminations' which the peasant was waiting for had already begun. Tar barrels were blazing right by the water's edge, creating huge bonfires. Their reflections, crimson as the rising moon, spread towards us in thick bands. The burning barrels illuminated their own smoke and the long shadows of people glimmering in the light; but further off to the side, and behind them, where the velvet sound of the bell was coming from, was the same impenetrable black darkness. Suddenly a rocket soared into the sky in a golden ribbon, cutting through the darkness; it made an arc and then with a bang exploded into sparks as if it had collided with the sky. From the bank came a rumble like a distant hooray.

'How beautiful!' I said.

'It certainly is!' sighed Ieronim. 'What a night, sir! Another time you might not pay attention to rockets, but today you rejoice over any bit of bustle. And where are you from?'

I said where I was from.

'I see… Today is a day of joy…' continued Ieronim in his feeble, halting tenor like a convalescing invalid. 'The sky, and the earth and the world below are all rejoicing. All creation is celebrating. But tell me, kind sir, why is it that even at times of such great joy a person cannot forget his sorrows?'

It felt like this unexpected question was an invitation to participate in one of those unbelievably protracted, soul-seeking conversations which bored and idle monks are enamoured of. I was not in the mood for talking much, so I simply asked:

'What are your sorrows, Father?'

'Usually the same as everybody else's, your honour, kind sir, but today a particular sorrow has befallen the monastery: Nikolay, our deacon, died right in the middle of the Liturgy, during the gospel reading…'

'Well, it's God's will!' I said, adopting a monastic tone. 'We all have to die. In my opinion, you should actually be rejoicing… They say that whoever dies just before Easter, or on Easter Sunday, will without fail go to heaven.'

'That's true.'

We fell silent. The silhouette of the peasant in the tall hat had fused with the outline of the river bank. The tar barrels were burning ever more fiercely.

'And the scriptures clearly point to the vanity of grief, and the importance of reflection,' said Ieronim, breaking the silence. 'But why does the heart ache and not want to listen to reason? Why do I want to weep bitter tears?'

Ieronim shrugged his shoulders, turned towards me and began to speak quickly:

'If it was me or someone else who died, it might not have been noticed, but it was Nikolay who died! No other person than Nikolay! It's hard even to imagine that he is not around any more! I've been standing here on the ferry, and I keep thinking his voice will sound from the other bank. He would always come down to the riverbank and call out to me, so that I wouldn't get frightened on the ferry. He would get out of bed at night specially to do it. A good soul! Goodness, how kind and good! Some people don't even have a mother like the friend I had in Nikolay! Lord save his soul!'

Ieronim took hold of the cable, but then immediately turned again to me.

'What a bright mind, your honour!' he said in a singing voice. 'And what melodious, sweet-sounding language! Just like what they are about to sing at matins: "O Beloved! O sweetest voice!" Apart from all the other human qualities, he had an exceptional talent too!'

'What was that?' I asked.

The monk looked at me, as if he had to verify first whether I could be trusted with secrets. Then he he laughed merrily.

'He had a gift for writing akathist[11] hymns...' he said. 'It was a real wonder, sir! You will be amazed when I explain it to you! Our archimandrite is from Moscow, his deputy graduated from the Kazan Academy, and we have various monks who are priests also, and elders, but blow me if any one of them can write, and here's Nikolay, a simple monk, a deacon, who didn't study anywhere, and wasn't even much to look at, but he could write! A wonder! A real wonder!'

Ieronim threw up his hands and continued enthusiastically, completely forgetting about the cable:

73

'Our deputy archimandrite finds it hard to write sermons, and when he was writing the history of the monastery, he wore all the brothers out, and had to go into town about ten times, but Nikolay just sat and wrote akathists! Akathists! It's not like writing a sermon or a history!'

'Are akathists difficult to write then?' I asked.

'Extremely difficult…' said Ieronim, twisting his head round. 'If God has not given you a gift, wisdom and holiness won't help you one bit. Monks who do not understand this think that you only need to know the life of the saint you are venerating, and take other akathists into account. But that's not right, sir. Obviously if you are writing an akathist, you need to know the life of the saint inside out, down to the last detail. And you also need to know about other akathists, so you know where to begin and what to write about. To give you an example, the first kontakion always starts with "victorious" or "chosen"… And you have to start the first ikos with an angel. The Akathist to Sweet Jesus, if you would be interested to know, begins: "Creator of Angels and Lord of Hosts", the Akathist to the Holy Virgin begins: "An Archangel was sent from heaven", the one to St Nikolay the Wonder-Worker begins: "An angel in manner, though earthly in nature", and so on. It always begins with an angel. Of course, it's not as if you don't have to have knowledge of other akathists, but, really, the main thing is not the life of the saint, or conformity with others, but beauty and melodiousness. Everything has to be elegant and concise but detailed. Every single line must be soothing, gentle, and tender; you can't have words which are crude, or harsh, and which don't fit in. You have to write so that the supplicant rejoices in his heart and weeps, while with his mind he trembles, and is filled with awe. In the Akathist to the Virgin there are the words "Rejoice, height inaccessible to human thoughts. Rejoice, depth invisible even to the eyes of angels!" In another place in that akathist are the words: "Rejoice, tree of delectable fruit that nourishes the faithful. Rejoice, well-shaded tree under which many find shelter!"'

Ieronim covered his face with his hands and shook his head, as if something had frightened him, or made him feel ashamed.

'"Tree of delectable fruit… well-shaded tree…"' he murmured. 'To be able to find words like that! That God may grant such a talent!

He would condense many words and thoughts into one word for brevity, but how smoothly and richly it came out with him! "Light-giving beacon of light shining…" it says in the Akathist to Sweet Jesus. Light-giving! There isn't a word like that in conversation or in books, he had to make it up, you know, find it in his head! Apart from smoothness and majesty, sir, every single line needs to be decorated in all kinds of ways, so that there are flowers, and lightning and wind, and sun, and all things in the visible world. And every exclamation has to be composed so that it is pleasant and natural for the ear. "Rejoice, lily of celestial growth!" you find in the Akathist to Nikolay the Wonder Worker. Not just "Rejoice, celestial lily", but "lily of celestial growth"! It's pleasanter and sweeter for the ear. That is how Nikolay wrote! Exactly like that! I can't begin to express to you how he wrote!'

'Then in that case it is a pity he has died,' I said. 'However, Father, let's keep moving, or we will be late…'

Ieronim came back to earth, and ran over to the cable. On the bank all the bells were beginning to be rung. The procession with the cross near the monastery had probably already started, because the whole dark space beyond the tar barrels was now sprinkled with moving lights.

'Did Nikolay ever publish his akathists?' I asked Ieronim.

'Where could he publish them?' he replied with a sigh. 'And it would have been strange to publish them. What would be the point? No one is interested in that in our monastery. They don't like it. They knew that Nikolay wrote, but they didn't pay it any attention. No one respects new writing these days, sir!'

'They were prejudiced against him?'

'Exactly. If Nikolay had been an elder, maybe the brothers would have taken an interest, but he wasn't even forty years old. There were some who laughed, and even considered his writing to be a sin.'

'Why did he write then?'

'More for his own consolation. I was the only one of the brothers who ever read his akathists. I would come and see him on the quiet, so others wouldn't see, and he was glad I was interested. He would embrace me, stroke my head, and say affectionate words, as if I was a small child. He would shut his cell door, sit me down next to him and start reading…'

Ieronim put down the cable and came over to me.

'We were sort of like friends,' he whispered, looking at me with shining eyes. 'Wherever he went, I would follow. And he would miss me when I wasn't around. And he loved me more than the others, but it was all because his akathists made me cry. It's moving to think about it! Now I am just like an orphan or a widow. You know, the people in our monastery are all good, and kind, and devout, but... none of them have subtlety and tact, they're just like simple people. They all talk loudly, their feet make a racket when they are walking about, they cough, they are noisy, but Nikolay always spoke quietly and gently, and if he noticed someone sleeping or praying he would walk past as quiet as a little fly or a mosquito. He had a compassionate, warm face...'

Ieronim sighed deeply and took hold of the cable. We were already approaching the bank. We had gradually floated straight from the darkness and the silence of the river into an enchanted kingdom, full of suffocating smoke, blinding light and din. Near the tar barrels you could now clearly see people moving. The glow from the fire gave their red faces and bodies a strange, almost fantastic expression. Horses' muzzles appeared occasionally amongst the heads and faces, as motionless as if cast in copper.

'They are going to sing the Easter canon now...' said Ieronim; 'and there's no Nikolay, no one to penetrate its meaning... For him there was no writing more beautiful than this canon. He used to understand the meaning of every word! When you are there now, sir, make sure you think about the meaning of what is being sung: it takes your breath away!'

'But aren't you going to be in church?'

'I can't go... I've got to work the ferry.'

'But won't they replace you?'

'I don't know... I should have been replaced after eight, but as you can see, I haven't been!.. I would like to be in church, to be honest...'

'Are you a monk?'

'Yes, sir... well, I'm a novice.'

The ferry ran into the bank and stopped. I slipped Ieronim five kopecks for the crossing and jumped on to land. A boy and a sleeping woman in a squeaky cart drove immediately on to the ferry. Tinged with red from the bonfires, Ieronim leant on the cable, bent over, and got the ferry moving…

I walked a little way through mud, but then found myself on a soft, newly trodden path. This path led through clouds of smoke, and a disorderly crowd of people, unharnessed horses, carts and carriages, to the dark and cavernous monastery gates. Flickering with crimson light and undulating shadows from the smoke, everything was squeaking, snorting, and laughing… Utter chaos! And people still managed to find room in all this scrum to load a small cannon and sell gingerbread!

On the other side of the wall, within the monastery, there was just as much bustle, except more order and decorum could be observed. There was a smell of juniper and incense here. The conversations were loud, but you could not hear any laughing or snorting. There were huddles of people with Easter cakes and bundles by the gravestones and the crosses. Many of them had clearly come from a long way away to have their Easter cakes blessed, and were now exhausted. Young novices were scurrying up and down the iron flags which lay in a long strip from the gates to the church doors, their boots clattering sonorously. There was also a great deal of toing and froing and shouting going on in the bell tower.

'What a restless night!' I thought. 'How wonderful!'

I wanted to see this commotion and sleeplessness expressed in all of nature, beginning with the darkness of the night, and ending with the iron flags, the graveside crosses, and the trees under which people were bustling about. But nowhere did all the excitement and commotion express itself more intensely than in the church. There was an unrelenting struggle going on in the doorway between the ebb and flow of people. Some people were coming in, and others were going out and then shortly afterwards coming back in again, in order to stand for a while and then once again start moving. People were darting about from one place to another, and then hanging around, as if they were looking for something. The wave went from the entrance and ran all the way through the church, affecting even the front rows, where the most respectable and important people were standing. There could be no question of concentrated prayer. In fact there was no prayer at all, but a kind of uniform joy, irrepressible and childlike, which was seeking

77

any excuse to burst out into the open and manifest itself in some kind of physical movement, even if only in the unforgiveable meandering about, and the crush.

The same extraordinary mobility was noticeable in the Easter service itself. The Royal Doors had been flung open in all the side-chapels, and thick clouds of smoke from the incense hung in the air around the main chandelier; wherever you looked there were bright lights and spluttering candles… There could be no question of readings; instead there was lively, high-spirited singing, unbroken until the very end of the service, with the clergy changing their vestments and shaking the censer after every song in the canon, which happened about every ten minutes.

I had barely managed to find a place to stand when a wave from the front surged and threw me back. A tall, well-built deacon with a long red candle walked by in front of me; the grey-haired archimandrite in his golden mitre hurried after him with the censer. When they had disappeared from view, the crowd squashed me back into my previous place. But barely ten minutes had gone by when a new wave surged, and the deacon appeared again. Behind him this time came the deputy archimandrite – the one writing the history of the monastery according to Ieronim.

As I fused with the crowd and became infected by the general jubilant excitement, I felt unbearably sad about Ieronim. Why could they not replace him? Why not put on the ferry a less sensitive, less impressionable person?

'Lift your Eyes Around You, Sion, and See…' the choir was singing; 'For Behold, like Beacons Shedding Light Divine, your Children have Come to You, from West and North, from the Sea and from the East…'

I looked at the faces. They all bore lively, festive expressions; but not one person was really listening and thinking about what was being sung; I could not see anyone's 'breath being taken away'. Why could they not replace Ieronim? I could imagine the fellow standing meekly somewhere over by the wall, his head bowed, keenly appreciating the beauty of every sacred phrase. With his sensitive soul, he would have eagerly drunk in everything that now was going over the heads of the people standing near me; he would have become intoxicated to the point of rapture, till his breath was taken away, and there would be no happier person in the whole church. But he was still shuttling back and forth on the dark river, and mourning his dead friend, the monk.

The wave surged behind me. A beaming, corpulent monk, fingering his rosary beads and looking back as he walked, elbowed his way past me as he cleared a path for some lady or other in a hat and a velvet coat. A lay brother from the monastery hastened to follow the lady, carrying a chair above our heads.

I left the church. I wanted to see the dead Nikolay, the unknown composer of akathists.

I strolled near the edge of the monastery, where a row of monastic cells stretched along the wall, peered in through a few windows, and turned back after not seeing anything. Now I do not regret not seeing Nikolay – heaven knows, maybe if I had seen him, it might have destroyed the image of him I had conjured up in my imagination. That kind, poetic man, in my mind's eye, lonely and misunderstood, coming out at night to exchange greetings with Ieronim, and sprinkling his akathists with flowers, stars and sunbeams, was pale and shy, with a gentle, diffident and wistful-looking face. And the kindness and barely repressible, childlike enthusiasm which I heard in Ieronim's voice when he produced those quotations from the akathists for me, must have also shone in his eyes and graced his thoughts.

When we left the church after the liturgy, it was no longer nighttime. Morning was beginning. The stars were extinguished and the sky was grey-blue and overcast. The iron flags, the gravestones, and the buds on the trees were covered with dew. A sharp freshness could be felt in the air. There was no trace of the commotion I had seen during the night outside the monastery. The horses and people were hardly moving, and seemed worn out and sleepy, while only a few handfuls of ash remained from the tar barrels. A person who is worn out and wants to sleep often thinks nature is in the same state. So it seemed to me that the trees and the young grass were now fast asleep, and that even the bells were not ringing as loudly and as joyfully as during the night. The commotion had finished and all that remained from the excitement was a pleasant weariness, and a desire for sleep and warmth.

I could see both banks of the river now. Above it there was a light mist hovering over the hills here and there. The water exuded a cold severity. When I jumped on to the ferry, someone's carriage and a few dozen men and women were already standing on it. The cable, which was damp and sleepy, or so it seemed to me, stretched far across the wide river and in places disappeared into the white mist.

'Christ is risen! No one else?' asked a quiet voice.

I recognised Ieronim's voice. Now the darkness of the night no longer prevented me from looking closely at the monk. He was a tall, narrow-shouldered man of about thirty-five, with a round face and prominent features, half-closed, lazy-looking eyes and an unkempt, wedge-shaped little beard. He looked unbelievably sad and tired.

'They still haven't replaced you?' I asked in amazement.

'Replace me?' he asked in return, turning his frozen, dew-covered face to me and smiling. 'There will be no one to replace me until morning now. They are all going over to the archimandrite to break the fast.'

He and some little peasant in a reddish-coloured fur hat shaped like the limewood tubs in which they sell honey, leant on the cable and grunted amiably, and the ferry moved off.

We floated along, disturbing lazy whisps of mist as we went. Everyone was silent. Ieronim worked the cable absent-mindedly with one hand. He surveyed us for a long time with his meek, dull eyes, then rested his gaze on the pink, black-browed face of a young merchant woman who was standing next to me on the ferry, and silently shivering from the mist enveloping her. He did not take his eyes off her the whole way over.

In that protracted gaze there was little that was male. It seemed to me that Ieronim was seeking in the woman's face the soft and gentle features of his dead friend.

A TALE

*dedicated to the moron who boasts about
being a newspaper contributor*

A fly was flitting from room to room and boasting loudly about writing for the newspapers.

'I am a writer! I am a journalist!' she buzzed. 'Make way, ignoramuses!'

Hearing this, all the mosquitoes, cockroaches, bedbugs and fleas were filled with respect for her, and many even invited her to lunch and lent her money, while the spider, who was afraid of *glasnost*, hid in the corner and decided not to cross paths with the fly…

'And what newspapers do you write for, Musca Ivanovna?'[12] asked the mosquito, who was bolder.

'Almost all of them! There are even newspapers to which I give nuance, tone, and even direction by virtue of my personal involvement… Without me, many newspapers would not have any character!'

'What do you write in the newspapers, Musca Ivanovna?'

'I have my own column…'

'Which one?'

'This one!'

And the journalist fly pointed to the countless dots with which the flyblown newspaper page was covered.

If one were to give all living Russian writers ranks corresponding to their talents and merits, this is what would result:[13]

Actual Privy Councillors: vacant.

Privy Councillors: Lev Tolstoy, Goncharov.

Actual State Councillors: Saltykov-Shchedrin, Grigorovich.

Civil Councillors: Ostrovsky, Leskov, Polonsky.

Collegiate Councillors: Maikov, Suvorin, Garshin, Burenin, Sergey Maksimov, Gleb Uspensky, Katkov, Pypin, Pleshcheyev.

Court Councillors: Korolenko, Skabichevsky, Averkiev, Boborykin, Gorbunov, Count Salias, Danilevsky, Muravlin, Vasilevsky, Nadson, N. Mikhailovsky.

Collegiate Assessors: Minaev, Mordovtsev, Avseyenko, Nezlobin, A. Mikhailov, Palmin, Trefolev, Pyotr Veinberg, Salov.

Titular Councillors: Albov, Barantsevich, Mikhnevich Zlatovratsky, Shpazhinsky, Sergey Atava, Chuiko, Meshchersky, Ivanov-Klassik, Vasily Nemirovich-Danchenko.

Collegiate Secretaries: Frug, Apukhtin, Vsevolod Solovyov, V. Krylov, Yurev, Golenishchev-Kutuzov, Ertel, K. Sluchevsky.

Gubernial Secretaries: Notovich, Maksim Belinsky, Nevezhin, Karazin, Vengerov, Nefedov.

Collegiate Registrars: Minsky, Trofimov, F. Berg, Myasnitsky, Linyov, Zasodimsky, Bazhin.

Without rank: Okreits.

The musician Smychkov[14] was walking from town to Prince Bibulov's dacha, where by prior agreement an evening of music and dancing would be 'laid on'. On his back he carried a huge double bass in a leather case. Smychkov was walking along the bank of the river, whose cool waters were flowing quite poetically if not majestically.

'What about a dip?' he thought.

Without further ado, he got undressed and lowered his body into the cool currents. It was a glorious evening and Smychkov's poetic soul started to tune into the harmonies of his surroundings. But that was nothing compared to the mellifluous feelings which enveloped him after he had swum about a hundred strokes and espied a beautiful girl sitting on the steep bank with a fishing rod in her hands. He held his breath and was deluged by a flood of disparate feelings: memories of childhood, nostalgia for the past, awakening love… Goodness, and he had thought that he would never be able to love again! After he had lost his faith in mankind (his dearly beloved wife had run off with his friend Sobakin, the bassoonist), his heart had been filled with emptiness, and he had become a misanthrope.

'What is life?' he had wondered often. 'Why do we live? Life is just myth, a dream… a ventriloquy act…'

But as he stood in front of the beautiful girl (it was not difficult to notice that she was asleep), he suddenly felt in his soul, against his will, something akin to love. He stood there in front of her for a long time, devouring her with his eyes…

'Well, enough of that…' he thought, letting out a deep sigh. 'Farewell, fair vision! Time for me to go to his excellency's ball…'

And after taking one last look at the beautiful girl, he was about to swim back, when an idea suddenly flashed into his mind.

'I should leave her something to remember me by!' he thought. 'I know! I'll attach something to her fishing rod. It will be a surprise from "a stranger".'

Smychkov swam carefully up to the bank, picked a large bunch of flowers from the meadow and the water's edge, bound it with a goose-foot stalk, and attached it to the line.

The bouquet sank to the bottom, taking with it the beautiful float.

Prudence, the laws of nature and my hero's social position demand that this romance finishes right at this very point, but – alas! – the author's fate is inexorable: for reasons beyond the control of the author, the romance did not end with the bouquet. Against all the laws of nature and common sense, the poor and undistinguished double bass player was destined to play an important role in the life of the rich and distinguished beautiful girl.

When he swam up to the bank, Smychkov was shocked: he could not see his clothes. They had been stolen... While he had been admiring the beautiful girl, unknown villains had stolen everything except his double bass and his top hat.

'Curses!' exclaimed Smychkov. 'Oh humans, offspring of viper! I'm not so bothered by being divested of my clothes (for clothes are perishable) as by the thought that I will now have to walk along starkers, and so infringe public morality.'

He sat on his double bass case and started to think about finding a way out of his terrible situation.

'I can't go to Prince Bibulov's naked!' he thought. 'There will be ladies there! Moreover, along with my trousers, the thieves have stolen the rosin which was in them!'

He agonised for such a long time that his temples started to hurt.

'Aha!' he remembered finally. 'Not far from the bank there is a little bridge in the bushes... I can sit under the little bridge until it gets dark, and in the evening, when dusk falls, I will make off to the first izba...'

Settling on this idea, Smychkov put on his top hat, hauled his double bass on to his back and trudged off towards the bushes. Naked, and with the musical instrument on his back, he looked like some ancient mythological demigod.

Now, reader, while my hero is sitting under the bridge and giving in to his sorrow, we shall leave him for a while and turn to the girl fishing. What happened to her? When she woke up and did not see her float on the water, the beautiful girl started pulling hurriedly on her line. The line tugged, but the hook and the float did not pop out of the water. Smychkov's bouquet had clearly become completely sodden and heavy, and had swelled up.

84

'Either I've caught a big fish,' thought the girl, 'or my line has caught on something.'

After tugging a bit more on the line, the girl decided that the hook had got caught.

'What a pity!' she thought. 'The fish bite so well in the evening! What shall I do?'

After pondering for a while, the eccentric girl cast off her ethereal clothes and lowered her beautiful body into the waters up until her marble shoulders. It was not easy to detach the line from the bouquet, which the line had got tangled up in, but patience and hard work paid off. About a quarter of an hour later, the beautiful girl emerged from the water with the hook in her hand, radiant and happy.

But evil fate had been lying in wait for her. The scoundrels who had stolen Smychkov's clothes now made off with her dress, leaving her with only her tin of maggots.

'What am I to do now?' she thought, as she burst into tears. 'Am I really going to have to set off like this? No, never! I'd rather die! I will wait until it gets dark, and then, under shadow of darkness I will go to old Auntie Agafya, and send her off home to get a dress for me… And meanwhile I'll go and hide under that little bridge.'

So my heroine ran over to the little bridge, taking care to choose grass that was taller, and bending down. As she crept under the bridge, she caught sight of a naked man with a hairy chest and a musician's shaggy mane, upon which she shrieked and fainted.

Smychkov also took fright. At first he had taken the girl for a nymph.

'Is this some river siren come to lead me astray?' he thought, and this conjecture flattered his ego, since he had always had a high opinion of his physical appearance. 'But if she is not a siren, but a person, how to explain this strange metamorphosis? Why is she here under the bridge? And what's the matter with her?'

While he was pondering these questions, the beautiful girl came round.

'Don't kill me!' she whispered. 'I am Princess Bibulova. I beg you! You'll be paid handsomely! I was just undoing my hook, and some thieves stole my new dress, my boots and everything!'

'Madam!' said Smychkov in an imploring voice. 'My clothes have been stolen too. Moreover, they not only swiped my trousers, but also the rosin which was in them!'

People who play the double bass and the trombone are not usually resourceful; Smychkov was a pleasant exception.

'Madam!' he said after a while. 'I can see that my appearance upsets you. But you must surely agree that I cannot leave this place for the same reason as you cannot. But here is what I have thought up: what about lying in my double bass case and pulling the lid over? That would hide me from you…'

After saying this, Smychkov took out his double bass from the case. For a brief moment, as he gave up his case, he felt he was profaning sacred art, but his hesitation was short-lived. The beautiful girl lay down in the case and curled up in a ball, while he did up the straps and began to rejoice that nature had endowed him with such intelligence.

'Now you cannot see me, madam,' he said. 'Lie here and relax. When it becomes dark, I will take you to your parents' house. I can come and pick up my double bass later.'

When night fell, Smychkov hauled the case with the beautiful girl in it on to his shoulders and set off for Bibulov's dacha. His initial plan was to get to the first cottage and find some clothing, and then go on further…

'Every cloud has a silver lining…' he thought, bending under his load, his bare feet kicking up clouds of dust. 'Bibulov will probably reward me handsomely for intervening in the princess' plight.'

'Are you comfortable, madam?' he asked in the tone of a *cavalier galant* inviting a lady to dance a quadrille. 'Please stretch out and make yourself at home in my case!'

Suddenly the gallant Smychkov sensed that there were two human figures veiled in darkness walking ahead of him. Looking closer, he verified that this was not an optical illusion: there were definitely two people walking along, and they were carrying some kind of bundles…

'I wonder if they are the thieves?' was the question which flashed into his mind. 'They are carrying something! It's probably our clothes!'

Smychkov put the case down by the side of the road and chased after the figures.

'Stop!' he shouted. 'Stop! Don't move!'

The figures looked round and then took to their heels when they saw they were being chased… For a long time the princess heard the sound of quick footsteps and shouts of 'stop!'. Then everything went silent.

Smychkov got embroiled in the chase, and probably the beautiful girl would have had to lie for a long time in the field by the road were it not for a fortunate coincidence. It so happened that Smychkov's friends, Zhuchkov the flautist and Razmakhaikin the clarinettist, were at that time walking along the same road on their way to Bibulov's dacha. When they stumbled across the case, they both looked at each other in surprise and threw up their hands.

'A double bass!' said Zhuchkov. 'Hey look, it's Smychkov's double bass! But how did it end up here?'

'Something must have happened to Smychkov,' decided Razmakhaikin. 'Either he got drunk, or he has been robbed… In any case, we can't just leave the double bass here. Let's take it with us!'

Zhuchkov hauled the case on to his back and the musicians carried on their way.

'It's damn heavy!' grumbled the flautist all the way. 'I wouldn't agree to play an old warrior like this in a million years… Ugh!'

When they arrived at Prince Bibulov's dacha, the musicians put the case down in the spot reserved for the band and set off to grab a bite to eat.

The chandeliers and wall-lamps were now being lit at the dacha. The bridegroom, court councillor Lakeyich, a handsome and attractive civil servant in the Ministry of Communications, was standing in the middle of the room with his hands in his pockets and chatting to Count Shkalikov. They were talking about music.

'You know, Count,' said Lakeyich, 'I became acquainted in Naples with a violinist who literally performed wonders. You wouldn't believe it! And on the double bass… on an ordinary double bass, he could play such devilish trills it was scary! He played Strauss waltzes!'

'Come on now, that's impossible…' said the count doubtfully.

'I promise you it's true! He even played the Liszt rhapsody! I shared a room with him, and I even learned how to play the Liszt rhapsody on the double bass, since I didn't have anything better to do.'

'The Liszt rhapsody… Hmm! You're kidding…'

'You don't believe me?' laughed Lakeyich. 'Well, I'll prove it right now! Let's go over to the orchestra.'

The bridegroom and the count headed over to the orchestra. They went up to the double bass, started quickly to undo the straps… and – horrors!

But while the reader gives free rein to his imagination in visualising how the musical argument resolved itself, let us turn to Smychkov… Having failed to catch the thieves, the poor musician did not find his valuable load when he returned to the place where he had left his case. Completely at a loss as to what to do, he paced up and down the road a few times, and when he did not find his case decided that he must be on the wrong road…

'This is terrible!' he thought, tearing at his hair and freezing with horror. 'She will suffocate in the case! I am a murderer!'

Smychkov walked up and down the roads until midnight looking for his case, but eventually became exhausted and so set off back to the bridge.

'I'll look at dawn,' he decided.

The searches at dawn had the same result and so Smychkov decided to wait for nightfall under the bridge…

'I will find her!' he murmured, taking off his top hat and tearing at his hair. 'Even if it takes me a year, I will find her!'

* * *

Even today peasants living in these parts will tell you that at nights near the bridge you can see a naked man in a top hat with overgrown hair. And just occasionally you can hear the wheezing sound of a double bass coming out from under the bridge.

SUPERFLUOUS PEOPLE

It is after six on a June evening. A crowd of dachniks who have just got off the train – mostly heads of households, weighed down by bags, briefcases and women's cardboard boxes – are plodding from the halt at Khilkovo towards the dacha village. They all look worn out, hungry and irritable, as if the sun never shines for them and the grass is never green.

Amongst those plodding along happens to be Pavel Matveyich Zaikin, member of the district court – a tall, stooping man in a cheap linen suit, and a cockade on his faded cap. He is red, sweaty, and despondent.

'Do you come out to your dacha every day?' a dachnik in red trousers asks him.

'No, not every day,' Zaikin replies glumly. 'My wife and son are living here permanently, but I come about twice a week. I don't have the time to come every day, and it's expensive too.'

'You're right about the cost,' sigh the red trousers. 'You can't get to the station in town on foot, you have to take a cab, then the train ticket costs forty-two kopecks… you buy a newspaper for the journey, and you give in and have a glass of vodka too. It's all kopecks, trifling sums, but you end up spending two hundred roubles over a summer if you're not careful. The bosom of nature of course has no price, there is no arguing that… it's idyllic and all that, but each kopeck has to be accounted for with our civil servants' pay, as you know. If you carelessly spend an extra kopeck somewhere, you don't sleep all night… Yes, indeed… I don't have the honour of knowing your name or patronymic, sir, but I earn almost two thousand a year, serve as a state councillor, smoke second-class tobacco, and do not even have a spare rouble to buy myself the Vichy mineral water I have been prescribed against kidney stones.'

'It's generally pretty loathsome,' says Zaikin after a short silence. 'I am of the opinion, sir, that it was devils and women who thought up life at the dacha. The devil was guided by spite, and woman by extreme thoughtlessness. For goodness sake, it's not life, but hard labour, hell! It's hot and humid here, it's difficult to breathe, and you wander from one place to the other like a lost soul, unable to find a refuge anywhere.

In the town, there is no furniture, and there aren't any servants… everything has been taken to the dacha… you feed on God only knows what, you can't drink tea because there is no one to heat the samovar, you don't wash, and then you come here, to this bosom of nature, and you have to walk in the dust, in the heat…. confound it! Are you married?'

'Yes, sir… three little ones,' say the red trousers with a sigh.

'It really is pretty loathsome… It's amazing we are still alive.'

The dachniks finally reach the village. Zaikin says goodbye to the red trousers and goes off to his dacha. At home he encounters complete silence. All you can hear are mosquitoes buzzing and a fly which has ended up as a spider's lunch. The windows are hung with muslin curtains through which you can see the pale red flowers of geraniums. Flies are dozing near the oleographs on the unpainted wood-panelled walls. There is not a soul in the hall, in the kitchen, or in the dining room. In the room which is simultaneously called the sitting room and the drawing room Zaikin finds his son Petya, a small six-year-old boy. Petya is sitting at the table, breathing heavily, with his lower lip sticking out as he cuts out a jack of diamonds with a pair of scissors.

'Oh, it's you Papa!' he says, without turning round. 'Hello!'

'Hello… Where's your mother?'

'Mama? She has gone with Olga Kirillovna to a theatre rehearsal. They've got a show the day after tomorrow. They're going to take me… Are you going?'

'Hmm… When is she coming back?'

'She said she would be back this evening.'

'And where's Natalya?'

'Mama took Natalya with her, so she could help dress her during the performance, and Akulina has gone into the forest to look for mushrooms. Papa, why do mosquitoes' stomachs turn red when they bite?'

'I don't know… It's because they are sucking blood. So no one is home?'

'No. I'm the only one here.'

Zaikin sits down in an armchair and looks blankly out of the window for a minute.

'Who is going to serve dinner?' he asks.

'They haven't cooked any dinner today, Papa! Mama didn't think you were going to come today, and didn't ask for dinner to be cooked. She and Olga Kirillovna are going to have dinner at rehearsals.'

'Wonderful. And what did you have to eat?'

'I had some milk. They bought some milk for me for six kopecks. Papa, why do mosquitoes suck blood?'

Zaikin suddenly feels something heavy approach his liver and begin to gnaw at it. He becomes so upset, annoyed and resentful that he starts trembling and breathing heavily; he wants to jump up, hit the floor with something heavy, and let off steam with a string of swear-words, but then he remembers that the doctors have strictly forbidden him to get over-excited, so he stands up, and forces himself to whistle a tune from *Les Huguenots*.

'Papa, can you act in the theatre?' he hears Petya's voice.

'Oh, stop bothering me with stupid questions!' says Zaikin angrily. 'You're clinging to me like a birch leaf in the bath house! You're six years old already, and you're still as stupid as you were three years ago… Stupid, spoilt child! Why are you ruining these cards for example? How dare you ruin them?'

'These cards aren't yours,' says Petya, turning round. 'Natalya gave them to me.'

'You're lying! You're lying, you wicked boy!' says Zaikin, getting more and more irritated. 'You're always lying! You should be spanked, you little swine! I'll box your ears!'

Petya jumps up, strains his neck, and gazes fixedly at the angry red face of his father. The boy's big eyes first blink, become clouded with moisture, and then his face crumples up.

'Why are you swearing?' Petya squeals. 'Why are you bothering me, idiot? I am not getting in anyone's way, I'm not being naughty, I'm being obedient, and you… just get angry! Why are you telling me off?'

The boy speaks convincingly, and he cries so bitterly that Zaikin feels ashamed.

'Really, why am I picking on him?' he thinks. 'Come now, that's enough…' he says, touching the boy on the shoulder. 'I'm sorry Petyukha… I'm to blame. You're a good boy, you really are, and I love you.'

Petya wipes his eyes with his sleeve, sits back down with a sigh and begins to cut out a queen. Zaikin goes into his study. He stretches out on the couch and with his hands beneath his head starts to think. The boy's recent tears have eased his anger, and he starts to feel relief from his liver. Now he just feels exhaustion and hunger.

'Papa!' Zaikin hears from behind the door. 'Do you want to see my insect collection?'

'Yes, show it to me!'

Petya comes into the study and gives his father a long green box. Without bringing it to his ear, Zaikin hears a desperate buzzing and scratching against the sides of the box. Lifting the lid, he sees a multitude of butterflies, beetles, grasshoppers and flies, all stuck to the bottom of the box with pins. With the exception of two or three butterflies, all of them are still alive and moving.

'The grasshopper is still alive!' says Petya in surprise. 'We caught him yesterday morning, and he hasn't died yet!'

'Who taught you to pin them?' asks Zaikin.

'Olga Kirillovna.'

'Olga Kirillovna should be pinned like that too!' says Zaikin with disgust. 'Take it away! It's shameful to torture living creatures!'

'Goodness, how poorly he is being brought up,' he thinks, as Petya leaves.

Pavel Matveyich has already forgotten about exhaustion and hunger, and is thinking only of his boy's future. Beyond the windows meanwhile, the daylight is slowly fading. You can hear groups of dachniks coming back from their evening swim. Someone stops near the open window of the dining room and shouts: 'Do you want any mushrooms?' – and then shuffles off barefoot when there is no response... But when the dusk thickens so that the geraniums lose their outline behind the muslin curtains, and the freshness of evening begins to seep in through the window, the door in the hallway opens noisily, and quick footsteps, talking, and laughter can be heard...

'Mama!' screams Petya.

Zaikin peers out of the study and sees his wife Nadezhda Stepanovna, pink-cheeked and blooming as always... With her is Olga Kirillovna, a dreary blonde with big freckles, and two unknown men: one is young and thin, with curly ginger hair and a big adam's apple, and the other is short and stocky, with a shaved actor's face and a blue-grey chin.

'Natalya, put on the samovar!' shouts Nadezhda Stepanovna, her dress rustling loudly. 'Apparently Pavel Matveyich has arrived! Pavel, where are you? Oh, hello Pavel!' she says, running into the study, and breathing heavily. 'You've come? I'm so glad… Two of my fellow amateurs have come back with me… come along, I'll introduce you… The tall one here is Koromyslov… he has a wonderful voice, and the other, the short one… is Smerkalov, a real actor… he reads magnificently. Ugh, I'm exhausted! We had a rehearsal today… It's going wonderfully. We are staging "The Lodger with the Trombone" and "She Awaits Him". The show is the day after tomorrow…'

'Why did you bring them back with you?' asks Zaikin.

'I had to, sweetheart! After tea we need to go over our roles and sing through some stuff… I'm going to sing a duet with Koromyslov… Oh, and how could I forget! Send Natalya to get some sardines, vodka, cheese and a few other things, dearest. They are probably going to stay on to supper… Oh, I'm so tired!'

'Hmm, I don't have any money!'

'That's no good, sweetheart! It would be embarrassing! Don't make me blush!'

Half an hour later Natalya is sent for vodka and snacks. Having had some tea and eaten a whole baguette, Zaikin goes into the bedroom and lies down on the bed, while Nadezhda Stepanovna and her guests start rehearsing their roles, making a lot of noise and laughing. Pavel Matveyich can hear Koromyslov's nasal singing and Smerkalov's dramatic exclamations for a long time… After the reading comes a lengthy conversation, punctuated by peals of laughter from Olga Kirillovna. Exercising his rights as a real actor, Smerkalov is explaining the roles with aplomb and fervour…

Then comes the duet, and the tinkling of china after the duet… Zaikin can hear them in his sleep persuading Smerkalov to read 'The Sinner', and then him giving in and starting to declaim. He hisses, beats his chest, cries, laughs in a hoarse bass… Zaikin frowns and burrows under the blanket.

'You've got a long way to go and it's late,' he hears Nadezhda Stepanovna's voice an hour later. 'Why don't you stay the night with us? Koromyslov can sleep here in the sitting room on the couch, and you Smerkalov, can have Petya's bed... We can put Petya in my husband's study... Really, why don't you stay?'

Finally, when the clock strikes two, everything falls silent... The bedroom door opens and Nadezhda Stepanovna appears.

'Pavel, are you asleep?' she whispers.

'No. Why?'

'Go and sleep on the couch in your study, dear, and I'll put Olga Kirillovna in your bed. Come on, dearest! I'd put her in the study, but she is frightened of sleeping alone... Come on, get up!'

Zaikin gets up, throws his dressing gown on, and shuffles into the study with his pillow... Feeling his way to his couch, he lights a match and sees Petya lying on it. The boy is not sleeping and is looking with big eyes at the match.

'Papa, why don't mosquitoes sleep at night?' he asks.

'Because... because...' mumbles Zaikin; 'Because you and I are superfluous here... There isn't even anywhere to sleep!'

'Papa, why does Olga Kirillovna have freckles?'

'Oh, shut up! I've had enough!'

After thinking for a while, Zaikin gets dressed and goes outside for some fresh air... He looks at the morning sky, at the motionless clouds, hears the lazy call of a sleepy corncrake, and begins to dream about the next day, when having gone back to town and come back from the court he will finally be able to collapse into bed... Suddenly a human figure appears from round the corner.

'Must be the nightwatch...' thinks Zaikin.

But looking and going up closer, he recognises the figure of yesterday's dachnik in the red trousers.

'You're not asleep?' he asks.

'No, can't sleep for some reason...' sigh the red trousers. 'I'm enjoying nature instead... You know, a guest arrived at our house on the night train... my wife's mama. My nieces arrived with her... lovely girls. I'm jolly glad, although... it's a bit nippy! And are you also enjoying nature, may I ask?'

'Yes,' mumbles Zaikin; 'I'm also enjoying nature… You don't happen to know if there is a tavern or an inn anywhere round here?'

Red trousers lifts his eyes to the sky and starts pondering deeply…

1899 REVISED VERSION OF *A LITTLE JOKE* WITH A DIFFERENT ENDING

A clear winter midday… The frost is hard and crisp, and Nadenka, who is holding my hand, has a silvery layer coating the curls on her temples and the down on her upper lip. We are standing on top of a big hill. From our feet down to the ground below stretches a sloping run, which the sun is looking at, as if it was a mirror. Near us are little toboggans upholstered in bright red cloth.

'Let's toboggan down, Nadezhda Petrovna!' I beg her. 'Just once! I promise you, we won't come to any harm, we'll be fine.'

But Nadenka is scared. As far as she is concerned, the entire slope from her little galoshes to the bottom of the toboggan run is an awful and unbelievably deep abyss. She is struck with fear and holding her breath as she gazes down, when I am merely suggesting that she sit down on a toboggan, but just think what might happen if she were to risk flying off into the abyss! She might die or go mad.

'Please say yes!' I say. 'You don't need to be scared! Come on, don't be such a coward!'

Nadenka finally gives in, and from her face I can see that she is giving in while fearing for her life. I sit her down on the toboggan, all pale and trembling, put my arm round her and then push off with her into the depths. The toboggan flies like a bullet. The air we cut through hits our faces and roars, whistles in our ears and roars, pinches us spitefully and painfully, and seems to want to tear our heads from our shoulders. The wind is so strong we can barely breathe. It seems as if the devil himself has grabbed us with his claws and is dragging us down to hell with a roar. Everything around us melts into one long strip that is tearing along at great speed… One moment more and it seems that we will perish!

'I love you, Nadya!' I say in a low voice. The toboggan starts travelling more and more quietly, the roar of the wind and the humming of the runners are no longer so frightening, it becomes easier to breathe, and then finally we are at the bottom. Nadenka is neither dead nor alive. She is pale and can scarcely breathe… I help her to stand up.

'Nothing in the world will make me do that again,' she says, looking at me with wide eyes full of terror. 'I promise you, I almost died!'

A little later she has recovered and is already looking beseechingly at me: did I really utter those four words or did she just hear them in the noise of the wind whooshing past? But I just stand there next to her, smoking and carefully examining my glove.

She takes my arm and we spend a long time walking around the hill. The mystery is clearly bothering her... Were those words said or not? Yes or no? Yes or no? It is a question of dignity, honour, life, happiness, a very important question, the most important in the whole world. Nadenka is impatiently and sorrowfully looking into my eyes and answering distractedly, while she waits to see whether I am going to start talking. Oh, the play of emotions on that sweet face, my goodness me! I can see that she is battling with herself, that she needs to say something, and ask some questions, but she cannot find the words, she feels awkward and scared, and it is getting in the way of her happiness...

'You know what?' she says without looking at me.

'What?' I ask.

'Let's do it again... go down in the toboggan.'

We walk up the steps to the top of the hill. Once more I settle the pale and trembling Nadenka on to the toboggan, and once again we fly into the terrible abyss; once again the wind roars and the runners start throbbing, and again at the fastest and noisiest point of our ride, I say in a low voice: 'I love you, Nadenka!' When the toboggan comes to a halt, Nadenka looks up at the hill which we have just come down, then looks intently at me while listening to my indifferent and dispassionate voice, and the whole of her little figure – every bit of it, even her muff and her hood – is an expression of utter bewilderment. On her face is written:

'What is going on? Who said *those* words? Was it him, or did I just hear them?'

The lack of an answer is annoying her and taxing her patience. The poor girl does not answer my questions, is frowning and on the point of tears.

'Should we go home now?' I ask.

'Actually... I like this tobogganing,' she says, going red. 'Shall we go down again?'

She 'likes' doing these runs, and yet as she gets on to the toboggan she is pale and trembling as at the other times, and barely able to breathe she is so scared.

We go down a third time, and I can see her watching my face and following my lips. I put my handkerchief to my lips and cough, but when we are halfway down the run manage to utter:

'I love you, Nadya!'

So the mystery remains a mystery! Nadenka is silent, thinking about something… I take her home, and she tries to dawdle and walk slowly, waiting to see whether I will say those words to her. And I can see that she is suffering, and has to make an effort to stop herself from saying:

'It can't be the wind that said them! And I don't want it to be the wind that said them!'

The next morning I get a little note: 'If you are going tobogganing today, come by and pick me up. N.' And from then on I start going on runs every day with Nadenka, and as we fly down in the toboggan, I say in a low voice the same words:

'I love you, Nadya!'

Soon Nadenka becomes as addicted to this phrase as if it was alcohol or morphine. She cannot live without it. She is just as terrified going down the run as before, of course, but now the fear and danger lend a peculiar charm to the declaration of love – a declaration which is a mystery, and causes heartache just like before. There are also the same two suspects – the wind and I… Which one of us is declaring their love for her she does not know, but she clearly no longer cares; it does not matter what vessel one drinks out of when the only goal is to be drunk.

One day I decide to go tobogganing in the middle of the day by myself; amongst the crowd I see Nadenka approaching the hill and looking out for me… Then she goes timidly up the steps… It is scary for her being on her own, really scary! She is white as snow as she climbs up, and trembling as if she is going to her execution, but she goes up doggedly, without looking back. She has obviously decided to carry out the ultimate test: will she hear those wonderfully sweet words when I am not there? I see her sitting down on the toboggan, all pale, her mouth open with terror, then shutting her eyes, parting with the world forever and pushing off… 'Zzzzzz!' go the runners. Whether

Nadenka hears those words I do not know… All I see is her getting up from the toboggan looking weak and exhausted. And one can tell from her face that she herself cannot tell whether she heard anything or not. The terror of going down took away her ability to hear, distinguish sounds or understand…

But then March arrives… The sun becomes more affectionate… Our slope goes dark, loses its sparkle and finally melts. We give up tobogganing. There is nowhere for poor Nadenka to hear those words now, and in fact there is no one to say them, because there is no wind, and I am about to go to Petersburg – for a long time, probably for good.

About two days before my departure I find myself sitting in my garden in the dusk, and it so happens that my garden is separated from the grounds of Nadenka's house by a high fence studded with nails… It is still quite cold, there is still snow under the manure, and the trees are leafless, but there is already a whiff of spring and the rooks are cawing loudly as they settle for the night. I go up to the fence and spend a long while peering through the gap. I see Nadenka coming out on to the porch and looking sadly and longingly up at the sky… The spring wind is blowing straight into her pale, sorrowful face… It reminds her of the wind which used to roar on the toboggan run when she heard those four words, and her face becomes ever so forlorn, and a tear trickles down her cheek… The poor girl holds out both arms, as if entreating the wind to bring her those words again. And when the wind does start blowing, I say in a low voice: 'I love you, Nadya!'

Good gracious, look at what is happening to Nadenka! She gives a cry, a smile lights up her face, and she holds out her arms to the wind, looking radiant, happy and beautiful.

Meanwhile, I go off to pack…

That was a long time ago. Nadenka is now married (whether she wed by choice or not is irrelevant) to a secretary of the Board of Trustees for the Nobility, and she has three children now. She has not forgotten that we used to go tobogganing together, or that the wind carried the words 'I love you, Nadenka'. That is the happiest, most touching, and beautiful memory in her life…

As for me, I can no longer understand, now that I am older, why I uttered those words, and for what reason I played that little joke…

NOTES

1. Perekladin's name is deliberately comical: the verb *perekladivat'* implies moving something from place to place, in this case, paper-shuffling. It was the custom for civil service functionaries to sign greetings cards to their superiors over the Christmas period.

2. The imperial Order of St Stanislav, established in 1831, had three classes, the third being the lowest. The holder was entitled to wear a cross on a ribbon (width 2.6 cm) on his chest.

3. The Slavyansky Bazaar and the Hermitage were two of the best-known restaurants in Moscow in late imperial Russia. The first telephone exchange was established in Moscow in 1882.

4. The epigraph comes from the beginning of *Joseph's Lament*, one of the most well-known popular 'psalms' in Russia.

5. The Retired Collegiate Secretary's name, Lakhmatov, is very close to the adjective *lokhmatyi*, meaning shabby.

6. Joseph Capoul (1837–1924) was a handsome French tenor, who performed in opera-comique in Russia to great acclaim.

7. In the Orthodox Church, the *panikhida*, a special requiem service for the dead, is performed on the third, ninth and fortieth day after the death of a person, and again after six and twelve months. Thereafter it is performed annually, but may be requested, as in this story, by members of the family at other times.

8. Bliny are Russian pancakes made of yeast and buckwheat which date back to pagan times, when they were cooked to celebrate the end of winter, and seen as symbols of the sun. They were later adopted by the Russian Orthodox Church.

9. In 1885, the Volsk zemtsvo in Saratov province did in fact transfer the administration of all its primary schools to the clergy, reducing the amount of financial support, and expecting the remainder to be raised locally.

10. Petersburg newspapers informed readers of the arrival of rooks in the capital on 18th March.

11. Akathists are hymns of praise in the Orthodox Church usually dedicated to Jesus, the Virgin Mary, or particular saints. They contain thirteen parts, each of which has a *kontakion* and an *ikos*.

12. In the original, the heroine is called 'Mukha' – the Russian word for fly. The Latin name is used in this translation.

13. The Table of Ranks was introduced in 1722 by Peter I for the Civil Service, the Imperial Court and the military. The writers assigned to lower ranks by Chekhov have been largely forgotten.

14. Smychok's name is derived from the Russian word for bow (*smychok*). The bassonist's name is derived from the word for dog (*sobaka*).

PUBLICATION DATES

1. 'The Exclamation Mark (A Christmas Story)' [Vosklitsatel'ny Znak] *Oskolki*, 28th December 1885.

2. 'New Year Martyrs' [Novogodnie velikomucheniki] , *Oskolki*, 4th January 1886.

3. 'Competition' [Konkurs], *Oskolki*, 11th January 1886.

4. 'A Failure' [Neudacha], *Oskolki*, 11th January 1886.

5. 'On the Telephone' [U telefona], *Budil'nik*, 19th January 1886.

6. 'Kids' [Detvora], *Oskolki*, 20th January 1886.

7. 'Grief' [Toska], *Peterburgskaya gazeta*, 27th January 1886.

8. 'Conversation Between a Drunkard and a Sober Devil' [Beseda p'yanogo s trezvym chertom], *Oskolki*, 2nd February 1886.

9. 'The Requiem' [Panikhida], *Novoe vremya*, 15th February 1886.

10. 'Bliny' [Bliny], *Peterburgskaya gazeta*, 19th February 1886.

11. 'A Little Joke' [Shutochka], *Sverchok*, 12th March 1886.

12. 'In Springtime' [Vesnoi], *Peterburgskaya gazeta*, 4th March 1886.

13. 'A Nightmare' [Koshmar], *Novoe vremya*, 29th March 1886.

14. 'The Rook' [Grach], *Oskolki*, 29th March 1886.

15. 'Grisha' [Grisha], *Oskolki*, 5th April 1886.

16. 'On Easter Night' [Svatoyu noch'u], *Novoe vremya*, 13th April 1886.

17. 'A Tale' [Skazka], *Oskolki*, 3rd May 1886.

18. 'The Literary Table of Ranks' [Literaturnaya tabel' o rangakh], *Oskolki*, 10th May 1886.

19. 'Romance With Double Bass' [Roman s kontrabasom], *Oskolki*, 7th June 1886.

20. 'Superfluous People' [Lishnie lyudi], *Peterburgskaya gazeta*, 23rd June 1886.

21. 'A Little Joke' [Shutochka], Anton Chekhov, *Rasskazy*, vol. 2 (St Petersburg, 1900), pp. 206–11.

BIOGRAPHICAL NOTE

Anton Pavlovich Chekhov was born in Taganrog, Russia, in January 1860. The son of a grocer, he studied medicine in Moscow, where he began writing short stories and comic sketches. He also wrote often humorous one-act dramas, although it is for his later, more serious plays that he is celebrated. He began practising medicine in 1884, and in 1887 his first full-length play, *Ivanov* was produced in St Petersburg. In 1888 he won the Pushkin Prize for his short story collection *In the Twilight*. A keen humanitarian, Chekhov worked in a free clinic for peasants, assisting in famine and epidemic relief. After a disastrous first production of *The Seagull* in St Petersburg in 1896, Chekhov vowed never to write for the theatre again, but the Moscow Arts Theatre production of 1898 was a success, as was *Uncle Vanya* in 1899. *Three Sisters* (1901) and *The Cherry Orchard* (1904) followed.

Chekhov had known for some time that he was suffering from consumption but during the 1890s his condition worsened, and in 1897 he moved to the Crimea, travelling back to Moscow only to advise on his productions. In 1901 he married the actress Olga Knipper who played a number of his characters on stage. Chekhov's vastly innovative and influential prose and drama focus on what Maxim Gorky termed 'the tragedy of life's trivialities' – the unhappy and banal lifestyles of his Russian contemporaries. He died in July 1904 and was buried in Moscow.

Rosamund Bartlett has written widely on Russian literature, music and cultural history. Her books include *Chekhov: Scenes from a Life* (Free Press), and *Literary Russia: A Guide*, co-authored with Anna Benn, recently reissued by Duckworth. As a translator she published the first unexpurgated edition of Chekhov's correspondence for Penguin Classics (*Anton Chekhov: A Life in Letters*), and her Chekhov anthology for Oxford World's Classics, *About Love and Other Stories*, was shortlisted for the 2005 Weidenfeld Translation Prize.